The Road Home

By Andrew Baze

Max Publications

Table of Contents

Introduction – Read Me!

Dear Readers,

In this book, you'll notice something uncommon in most adventure novels: the use of **end notes**. These end notes are organized in the Bonus Content section, in the last chapter.

If you see a word with a small number next to it, flip to the Bonus Content section, look up that number, and you can learn more about that subject. Here are a couple examples: you can learn more about what most important things should be in your backpack when you go on a **hike**[1], or what **ham radio**[3] is.

Do you want more tips on ham radio, emergency communications, wilderness survival, disaster preparedness, and other neat topics? Go to **www.PreparedBlog.com**, and you can find more general tips, details about topics found in this book, pictures, links, and other cool stuff!

I hope you love the story and enjoy the extra details.

73,
-Andrew Baze
AB8L

1

Prologue

Robbie stopped running and wiped the sweat off his forehead. He breathed heavily and leaned forward with his hands on his thighs, trying to force more air into his lungs. He had to get to the truck, and this stupid mistake had cost him precious time.

In the back of his mind, a doubt surfaced. Would he be able to save his father's life? Had his mistake caused a delay that would somehow put his father in more danger? And what about his mother and sister?

Robbie shook his head and dismissed the doubt. He couldn't stop, and definitely couldn't give up. Everything would be OK. His mother and sister were probably fine, and his father would be out of danger soon. But he had to find his way back to the truck.

1. Heading Out

Robert Parker brushed his mussed, brown hair out of his eyes and stuffed two pairs of wool socks in his backpack. This was the first weekend in a long time that he and his dad had to themselves. They were going camping. No mom and sister — boys only. Robbie thought about all the fun things that they'd do. They'd be hiking, sleeping in a tent, building a fire, and one more especially interesting activity: using his new birthday present, a high-tech, handheld ham radio.

"Are you almost ready?" his father called from downstairs. "Get moving. The great outdoors is calling!"

"Yeah. I'll be down in a minute," Robbie called back.

Robbie picked up his backpack. It was heavier than he thought it would be. All those small, light items really added up. He shrugged on the pack and walked down the stairs as quickly as he could without falling down.

"I'm ready Dad. Let's go!"

"OK, but before we go, let's check out your pack. Did you pack everything you'll need?"

"Yep. Extra socks and underwear, three pairs of pants, six cans of beans and two cast-iron frying pans, just in case we lose one."

Jeff Parker stopped adjusting the shoulder strap on his pack and looked at his son sideways, with one eyebrow raised. "Are you sure that's what you're packing? Did you go through the checklist I gave you?"

"Hah — I totally got you with that one. Why would I bring a big, heavy frying pan — or two of them? I know better than that. I probably couldn't even carry that extra weight anyway."

Jeff smiled. "OK, you got me. Good one. I knew you were a smart boy. But now you get to prove it. Let's walk through what's in there. I'm sure you did a good job packing, but it won't hurt to double-check."

Robbie pulled a worn piece of paper out of this back pocked, unfolded it, and read. "Fire-starter, multi-tool, water, map and compass...," and continued through the list[1]. As he read each item, he pulled something out of his pack or pointed to something inside.

Robbie eventually reached the end of the list: "...extra socks and underwear and last but not least, my new radio, and extra batteries."

"Not bad, but you forgot a couple of things," Jeff said patiently. "Remember when I told you that being able to make a fire was one of the most important things you'll need to do if you're lost in the mountains?"

"Yeah, and I have my fire-starter — a lighter."

"Do you remember what I said about a backup plan?" Jeff had a blank look on his face. He always did this when he was quizzing Robbie and it was usually annoying.

"Dang it. Yeah," Robbie sighed. "I need another way to start a fire." He should have put that on his list. His dad had said it often enough.

"Yes, the most important things should be backed up. Here, take this. Since they're small, I had a couple extras." Jeff handed over a small, dark-colored metal rod that had a metal striker attached with a lanyard. It was ferrocerium[2], which was harder to use than a lighter, but good in other ways. "This is your backup fire-starter. What else is missing?"

"Um…" Robbie hesitated. What else had he forgotten? He thought he'd been thorough, but clearly he'd missed something. He gave up and shrugged, "I don't know."

"Think, Robbie. How are you going to purify water up there? The water in your bottle won't last the whole weekend, and if you drink from a stream or lake, you could get sick from bacteria or parasites."

"Oh yeah, water…"

Jeff rummaged around in a plastic bin next to him and pulled out a small bottle of Iodine tablets. "The water won't taste great, but it will be safe. Stick this in your bag. Don't worry — I have a pump water filter, so we can still have fresh-tasting water. Those tablets are just in case the pump breaks. And there's one more thing."

"I give up," Robbie said. "I have no idea."

"Don't worry," Jeff said, "nobody's perfect. I forgot to add water purification to the list when I gave it to you, so that one's my fault. And that reminds me how important the last thing is: your brain. Don't forget that if something bad happens, you have to think. If you can use your head while you deal with a problem, you'll be much better off."

"Fine. Can we be done with this please? Come on, Dad. We need to go." Robbie was getting impatient. He'd been ready to run out and have fun, and now his dad was grilling him when they could be on the road.

"OK," Jeff said. "Let's go. Oh, yeah — did you remember the manual for your radio? It might make for some light reading in the tent at night."

Robbie pulled it out of his jacket pocket and showed it to him without saying a word.

Jeff smiled. "Good." He knew Robbie occasionally got frustrated with his questions, but at the same time, Jeff knew he only had a few years left to teach Robbie as much as he could. At age 14, Robbie still had a lot to learn. Plus, Jeff wanted to make sure the manual was handy. That radio had so many features that neither of them knew how to use all the options.

The radio had been an early birthday present. Ever since Robbie had gotten his license and call sign a month ago, he had been eager to practice with Jeff's radio, so this was the perfect gift. Jeff had given it to him a month before his birthday so Robbie would have time to learn how to use it and get some practice before they went on their trip. It was a hand-held ham radio, about the size of a walkie-talkie commonly for sale at many outdoor sporting goods stores. But this radio was more powerful and much, much cooler[3].

Jeff had given Robbie a higher-end radio — a Yaesu VX-8R. This had previously been reviewed as one of the best handheld ham radios on the market, but there were newer models out now. Even so, this radio was compact, had good transmission power, and was loaded with more features than Robbie was able to understand or use yet. It could even use Bluetooth accessories!

Robbie had been excited about the early, unexpected gift, and had spent countless hours trying to memorize the many functions of the knobs and buttons. He repeatedly referred back to the manual, and sometimes had to ask his father for help. After a few days of checking out many of the radio's features and making some practice calls with Jeff, they sat down together so Robbie could talk with someone else. With butterflies in his stomach, Robbie turned up the power setting, pressed the "Transmit" button, and called out to see if anyone could hear him. Jeff sat next to him, ready to help if needed.

"This is KE7CTA," said Robbie. "KE7CTA" was his call sign[4], and he was required to say it at least every ten minutes when he talked on the radio while using any ham radio frequencies. He continued: "I'm a new ham, and checking to see if someone out there can hear me."

"KE7CTA, this is AB8L[5]", said a man's voice. "I'm in a truck on I-90, headed east, just outside of Bellevue. I read you loud and clear — your signal is strong. What's your location?"

"I'm in Bellevue," Robbie called back. "Thanks for the signal report — you sound clear, too. Have a great day."

"You too. AB8L clear."

"KE7CTA clear."

He did it! This was his first real communication with the outside world on the radio airwaves, and Robbie was excited. It felt like exploring uncharted territory. Now he could connect with people he didn't even know existed. It was like connecting with someone using an Internet chat or messaging program, except this didn't need a computer or a keyboard. And he was just getting started. Soon he'd be able to try something else. Once they were up in the mountains, he could try talking with his mother, who would be 70-80 miles away as the crow flies — they'd measured on a map earlier in the week. Hopefully he'd get that chance later today, if things went as planned.

Robbie was also interested to see how well the GPS [6] function worked. His radio had a GPS receiver built into the separate handheld microphone and speaker attached to with a flexible, coiled cable. He could use a service called "APRS"[7] to send out his location and other data. This transmission would bounce off other ham radio stations, which would re-transmit the data until it reached the radio at home, where his mother would be listening. At the same time, the coordinates would be automatically transmitted to a station connected to the Internet so a live map could be updated; his mother would be able to see where they were by checking a map with her computer. She would even be able to see them move. If the Internet wasn't available, she could put their coordinates into her computer map software, which would show her where they were.

This little radio was amazing. Not only could it transmit on several frequencies (different "bands" of frequencies), it could also send text messages using the APRS system. Robbie was always texting his friends and family with his cell phone, and was surprised to learn that he could text with his radio, too. It was amazing how much technology was packed into this device.

Jeff pointed at the radio clipped to the front of the shoulder strap on Robbie's backpack. "After all the time you spent figuring out how to use that thing, we'll have to make sure you get lots of practice with it when we're up in the mountains."

"Heck yeah," Robbie replied. "Can we go now?"

"OK. Let's do it," said Jeff. He pulled his pack onto his shoulder and headed toward the front door. Robbie had finished re-packing his bag and grabbed it by its straps. Jeff stopped to hug and kiss Robbie's mother, Marie. Before Robbie could bolt out the door, Marie caught him and gave him a big hug and kiss.

"Stay safe, boys," Marie said. "We women will guard the fort while you're out playing."

"We'll take good care of each other, sweetheart," Jeff replied. "Right, Robbie?"

"Yeah, sure. Bye." Robbie said over his shoulder as he walked toward the truck. He wanted to *go*.

"What time should I be listening for you guys on the radio?" Marie asked.

Jeff thought for a moment. "Give us an hour and a half or so, then start listening. We'll try calling using a repeater, so use memory channel three — I programmed it in last night. And then we'll do APRS, and you'll be able to see exactly where we are. For that, you can use the Internet map. It's in your favorites list, remember?

"Yeah. Sounds good," Marie replied. "I love you. I hope you have a great time."

"We will. I love you, too." Jeff gave Marie a quick kiss. He was looking forward to being out in the woods for a "guys' weekend", but at the same time he knew he'd miss the rest of his family.

Robbie loved his mom, but didn't have time for a long good-bye. He had already loaded his backpack into the back seat of the Chevy pickup truck's crew cab and was sitting in front. He clicked in his seatbelt. "Let's go, Dad! Time's a-wastin'."

"Let's do it," Jeff replied. He kissed Marie once more, and walked over to the truck. "We have a full tank of gas, full bellies, plenty of supplies, and it's a beautiful day."

Robbie reached into his jacket pocket and pulled his book on wilderness survival. He opened it to where he'd left off the night before, the section on knots. It was time to relax for the ride.

"Have fun!" called Marie, from the front porch. "Bye!" Robbie's five-year-old sister, Lisa, stood next to her mother, and stuck her tongue out at Robbie, then laughed and waved too. Since before either of them could remember, Robbie and Lisa had learned that waving when someone left was just something you did. They'd wave until the person leaving was all the way out of sight. It was a fun family ritual.

Robbie & Jeff continued to wave and smile at the girls as they pulled away and drove down the street. They didn't know then they were starting a day that nobody in the family would ever forget.

2. Going for a Walk

Luis woke up early. Actually, he woke to the sound of someone banging on a pan downstairs, the signal that coffee was ready and he was expected to get out of bed. For whatever reason, none of the residents at the halfway-house were ever allowed to sleep in, whether it was a weekday or not. Moments after Luis arrived, the old man running the place started his first of many lectures, saying something about "early to bed, early to rise…" And true to form, Luis had immediately started ignoring anything the man said, his thoughts drifting to plans for his newfound freedom: girls, pizza, beer and other trivialities.

The first day there, Luis decided to sleep in. He heard the banging-pan alarm, rolled over and went right back to sleep. Later that same morning, after he eventually got up, the same man who had lectured him the day before told him that if he didn't comply with house rules, his parole officer would be notified. Luis knew what that meant — there was a good possibility he'd be back in prison, and that was a bad plan.

The funny thing, he thought groggily as he pulled on his pants and t-shirt, was that the "freedom" of the halfway-house was still like being in prison. But he only had to stay here for another month or so, and then he'd be able to move on, be on his own again, and score some serious money, not the spare change he was earning at his mandatory, so-called "job."

Luis worked in a fast-food restaurant a short bus ride away. After only three weeks, he already hated it with a passion. It wasn't as bad as being in prison, but it wasn't as easy as committing a couple of thefts a week and converting the fruits of that labor to cash at the local pawn shops. Even at pennies on the dollar, the cash he got from stealing was a lot more than his pathetic paycheck.

There were three big problems with working at the restaurant. The first problem was the pay. After his first two weeks on the job, he got his first paycheck. He opened the unsealed envelope and pulled out the check. He had plans — a big dinner in a good restaurant, maybe a new MP3 player... Then he was confused. The number was too small. He flipped to the piece of paper that showed hours and other details, and there was a small number on the top that got even smaller when other numbers were subtracted. What the heck were all of these other numbers? In his nineteen years, he'd never had a legitimate job, so translating hours of work into cash was a new idea to him, and full of surprises. He had complained to the manager, who told him "Taxes, son. Ain't you ever heard of taxes? You got your FICA, and you got your Medicare, and you got..."

Of course, Luis didn't get tips either, so the end result was a wage he couldn't live on. Not unless he worked more shifts, anyway. Maybe it would be OK for a high school kid living at home, or someone who had another working family member. But once he moved out of the halfway-house and had to pay real rent, there was no way he would have enough left over to buy a car, or gas, food, beer, clothes, a flat-screen TV and DVD player, and other stuff he wanted.

The second problem was that he couldn't quit. When he'd asked his parole officer what his options were if he quit his job, he encountered yet another authority figure quick to laugh at him. His parole officer, an overweight man named Emilio, guffawed as he answered, so hard that his belly jiggled: "Sure, you can quit, boy. And you'll go right back to jail, with no possibility of parole for the remainder of your sentence." Yes, the parole people had told him earlier that keeping a job was a condition of his parole. Nobody had told him that the only option was a job he'd hate. Luis felt trapped. Even though he was out of prison, it felt like the system was still imprisoning him. He wanted his freedom back, and this situation was completely unfair.

The third problem with his job was the smell. Whether he was learning how to prepare the food in or just running the register, the smell clung to him as if it had been sprayed on like paint. The fryer grease, the spattering grill, chopping onions — they all magically combined into a foul odor that he couldn't get rid of. Even after taking a shower last night and another one this morning, he could still smell it…

Today wasn't as bad as other days, though. Today he was free. It was Saturday, a day off. He needed the fresh air and hoped for some sunshine to help clean the smell away. He often went on walks. It was the only way he could get out of the house without spending money.

Luis walked down the sidewalk, checking out each house he passed. He wasn't far from "home", so he was only window-shopping. In prison he'd learned some valuable lessons from his cell-mate and some other guys he'd befriended in the cell block. One of those lessons was to avoid committing any crimes near your home. Apparently one of the first things that the cops would do is look for any known parolees or criminals living nearby. The halfway-house would be one of their prime targets. He learned this from a guy who had actually been caught this way. At the time, Luis had committed the story to memory. He filed it under "How not to get caught". For now,

14

Luis was just practicing, looking at the houses he passed and asking himself "What if that house was empty?" It was a fun way to pass the time, because the houses in this neighborhood appeared to be in good condition. Luis enjoyed imagining "the perfect score": an empty house, a safe left open (because he had no idea how to open one), and a sack so full of money that he could barely carry it. From then on, it would be Easy Street for him — no more fast food job and no more worrying about how to buy what he wanted. He could even leave the state and start fresh somewhere else. He'd figure out what to do about his parole later, and he wasn't going to let that detail spoil his fantasy. Yes, there were some fine-looking houses in this neighborhood...

3. Driving and Hiking

Jeff drove eastward on Interstate 90, out of Bellevue, past the cities of Issaquah, Snoqualmie, and North Bend. The traffic in the opposite direction was getting heavier and heavier.

"Check it out," Jeff said. They passed three RV's in a row, apparently a small convoy, each with a fluttering flag attached to its radio antenna. "The big game is today."

The Seattle Mariners were playing in the last game of the playoffs starting at 1:00, and fans from across the state (and even neighboring states) had been flocking to the area starting the day before to get ready for the pre-game festivities. The Mariners had done much better this season than in previous years, and the games drew record crowds. Team spirit reached a new high when they made it to the playoffs, and most hotels in the area were packed to capacity. These were probably the last of the fans, if they wanted to get to the game on time.

"Yeah, I know," Robbie replied. Many of the boys in school had been talking about it all week. They talked about their favorite players, their statistics, how the home team would destroy the visiting team, etc. A few of them had bragged that they would be there, but Robbie wasn't worried about missing out. He had been planning on going on this trip with his dad long before the playoff teams were announced. He planned on having a lot more fun in the mountains, out in nature, trekking around like an explorer with his dad, knife on his belt and his home on his back. There was something about being in the outdoors and being on his own that appealed to him much more than a five-hour, slow-moving baseball game.

"Yeah, I'm glad we're going this way and not in that mess," Jeff said.

"Mm-hmm," Robbie replied absentmindedly, as he flipped through his radio manual.

"Half tank. Time to refill," said Jeff. He hadn't filled up the truck's gas tank before they left, and it was now half empty. Jeff pulled off at the next exit, into North Bend, to fill the gas tank the rest of the way. Based on Jeff's earlier calculations, they shouldn't have to worry about gas for the rest of the trip[8].

"Do you need anything to eat or drink?" Jeff asked as the gas pump clunked along, slowly filling the tank.

"Nah, I'm still full from breakfast." Robbie continued to flip through the manual, trying to understand more of the radio's long list of features.

Minutes later, Jeff twisted the gas cap shut, hopped in the driver's seat, and guided the truck back toward the highway.

"OK," Jeff said. "Let's check in quickly with your mother. I'm pretty sure we'll be able to send a message from here. It worked last year when I tried it. You can try it this time."

"Sure. We can use APRS, right? We can send a text message. I want to try that again."

"Yeah, that's a great idea. Let's try it out." Then Jeff smacked his hand on the steering wheel. "Dang it."

"What, Dad?"

"We don't have the antenna up. I totally forgot. Hold on while I get us off the road." He hadn't reached the on-ramp yet, and pulled into the parking area of a small strip-mall.

"I left the mag-mount antenna in the back here..."

Robbie knew that his dad was talking about the magnetically-mounted antenna because he'd seen him use it before. Robbie even knew why it was better than his radio's small antenna. Jeff had shown him a cool video of moving radio waves and what they did if someone used a hand-held radio inside a car or truck, versus using an antenna stuck to the top of a vehicle. If the regular, short antenna was used, the transmitted radio waves mostly bounced around inside the cab. Some of them made it out, and could be received by another radio in the area, but the range was much shorter than it could be. However, if an antenna was outside the vehicle, preferably on the top, much more of the radio's power was transmitted outward instead of bouncing around inside.

Jeff opened the driver side back door and was rummaging around behind the driver's seat. A moment later, he pulled out a flat, half-inch-thick disc with a cable coming out of the side. Then he pulled out a long, flexible, metal whip and screwed it onto the top of the base. The base contained a strong magnet that would keep the antenna firmly in place, even at highway speeds. Jeff stepped up onto the runner below his door, reached over the top of the cab, and placed the antenna in the center of the roof. It stuck with a *thunk*. The thin cable trailed down over the side of the truck's roof, and Jeff guided it around the back door gasket before shutting the door, making sure to not pinch the cable in the hinge. He handed the end of the cable to Robbie and got back in the truck.

"OK, hook it up and let's give it a shot. I'll keep driving." Jeff pulled out of the parking and one block later took the onramp to I-90, back on track.

Robbie unscrewed the "rubber duck" antenna (a commonly-used term for the short and usually inefficient factory antenna) from his radio, and screwed the cable connector in place. Now he could broadcast with the much more efficient antenna and should have a much clearer signal with more range.

He switched his radio to APRS mode and selected his mother's call sign from the list already programmed into the radio. He entered the characters of the text message using the radio's keypad: "We R OK, U?" Then he hit "send." It took more keystrokes than if he was using his cell phone, but it was manageable.

The radio waves containing the text message exited the antenna on the top of the truck at the speed of light, radiating in all directions away from the truck, more or less parallel with the ground. A microsecond later, they were picked up about 11 miles to the east by a radio sitting in the spare bedroom of a house belonging to a local ham radio operator.

This radio was left on 24 hours a day and was configured as a "digipeater" (digital repeater). It automatically re-transmitted the message, this time with more power and a more efficient antenna, mounted high on the house's chimney. The transmission was picked up by another station, about thirty miles east. This station was different than the first because it was also connected to the Internet. The radio, attached to a computer, was able to link to another Internet-connected digipeater all the way across the pass, near Bellevue. This final digipeater repeated the transmission one final time, and the information was received, seconds after it was transmitted, by the radio sitting in Jeff and Marie's living room.

A few minutes later, Robbie received a text message on his radio. "All OK. I C U!" His eyes lit up.

"Mom sees us, Dad! I bet she can see our truck on the Internet map. That's cool!"

"Yeah, that is cool. When we can reach an APRS digipeater connected to the Internet, anyone in the world can see our location."

"Sweet." Robbie texted back. "Got it - TTYL."

Minutes later, Robbie received another reply. "TTYL. Have fun!"

Robbie sat and grinned. This radio was so cool. He wondered how many other uses he would find for it. He thought about the possibilities as he picked up his manual with renewed interest. It was pretty technical, and some things were hard to understand, but he knew he'd be able to figure out most of them, especially with his father around to help.

About thirty minutes later, Jeff said: "Hey Robbie — how's that coming along?"

"Pretty good. There's some interesting stuff in here, but a lot of stuff I don't get. Did you know that there is a Morse code training option in this radio? Who would want that?"

"You might be surprised," Jeff replied. "There are still plenty of people who use it, even though it's not required for a license anymore."

"Sounds like a hassle to learn."

"It's not that hard. It takes a little practice, like anything new, but it's easier than you think. I'll show you how to learn it if you want. But you'll need to use a different radio. Not many people use Morse code with handheld radios."

"Hmmm… maybe later." Robbie flipped the page in his manual and kept reading.

They drove for a few more minutes in silence.

"I have an idea," Jeff said. "We just crossed Snoqualmie Pass. Soon we'll get to Easton. When we do, we'll need to get ready to head north when we get to Cle Elum. Could you check the map and give me directions as we go?"

"Sure," said Robbie, "I'll help navigate."

About 20 minutes later, they passed Easton.

"OK, time to help. How far out are we?"

Robbie put away the manual. He took the map from the center console where Jeff had set it. He guessed where they were and started looking for any exit or other road signs for confirmation.

He watched as the stands of trees and thick, green undergrowth gave way to open spaces dotted with pine and fir trees. Since there was less rain on the east side of the Cascade

Mountains, there was also less vegetation. As Robbie watched the terrain change, he thought about how it would be a lot less work to hike wherever they wanted, without necessarily having to stay only on trails. They would be able to "bushwhack" — blaze their own trail into the great unknown, without having to push through patches of blackberries or other thick brush.

Eventually, they passed the first exit sign for the town of Cle Elum, and Robbie found their position on the map. He kept track of their progress as they passed mile markers.

Eventually he got bored of staring out the window and waiting for the next sign, and he didn't understand the political discussion his dad was listening to on the radio. He took out a different map and looked it over. This was no ordinary roadmap. It was a topographical map[9], which showed the terrain in more detail. It had special lines that showed elevation at different points, and how steep the hills and mountains were.

The hiking route was marked on the map in pencil, and Robbie could tell that it would be a challenging hike to the campsite where they planned to stay for the first night. This leg of the trip would be just over four miles, and it crossed a lot of lines on the map, which meant that they would be going higher and higher. It would be a solid hike for the first half-day, and if they made good time, they'd still have plenty of time to set up camp and purify some water while they still had daylight. Robbie smiled to himself as he imagined being up in the mountains, making fire, finding water from a stream , cooking dinner, eating until he was stuffed, testing out his flashlight, looking at the stars... It was going to be cool.

Robbie also wondered whether he'd be able to make it. Although he had done a lot of running around and playing over the summer break, he'd also spent a lot of time watching TV, playing video games and reading. Would his legs be strong enough? Would he have to stop and take breaks all the time?

He didn't want to be a wimp in front of his dad, and he didn't want to slow down the hike.

"Robbie, see if we have any bars left on the cell phone. I want to give Mom a quick call before we're out of range."

Robbie picked up the cell phone from the truck's center console, and looked at the screen. No bars. They were already out of range.

"No bars, Dad."

"OK. We'll use the phone on our way back. In the meantime, I bet we can reach her with our radios using the repeater system. Let's try once we're up on the mountain."

About 15 minutes later they exited the Interstate and turned onto a side road. Another 15 minutes after that, they turned onto a forest service road and kept going. Jeff slowed down, bumping down the unpaved, poorly-maintained road. Sometimes it got so narrow that only one vehicle could fit at a time, so they approached slowly and drove cautiously. A head-on car crash up here could be fatal or at least life-threatening, and medical help was far away.

About a half hour later, they turned into a gravel parking area and pulled to the far end, near a small wooden sign that read "Red Horse Trail". Two other vehicles, a car and a compact pickup truck, were also parked in the lot, and Jeff parked a few yards away from them.

"OK, Robbie, this is it. From here we go on foot. Grab your gear and saddle up!"

"I forgot the horse, Dad," Robbie said as he stepped out of the truck.

"Funny, boy. You're the horse, and if you don't get moving, I'll saddle you with some of my gear, too," Jeff replied with a grin. "How would you like that?"

"OK, OK, I'm ready. Don't touch my pack. I have plenty of stuff already. Let's go!" The crisp, fresh mountain air was exhilarating, and they were starting an adventure. Robbie was itching to get going.

After Jeff locked the truck, they found the trailhead and started hiking away from the parking area. They made their way slowly along the side of the mountain, covered a long, flat stretch, and then started to gain elevation as they hiked along some shorter stretches that zigged and zagged up the side of the mountain.

"Switchbacks are a lot of work, Dad," Robbie groaned.

"Yeah," replied Jeff, "but they're a lot easier than trying to go straight up. Have you ever tried that? Trust me — it's more work than you would think. Here's another way to look at it. You could try lifting one really, really heavy weight once, and maybe you couldn't lift it because it's too heavy, or maybe you could barely lift it, but you might pull a muscle or something. That's no good. But if you could break that weight down into small chunks, you could easily lift them one at a time, without hurting yourself. Switchbacks break the climb into little chunks that are easy to handle. Count your blessings that we have these switchbacks."

Robbie's leg muscles burned from the exertion for a short while, but he eventually got used to the pace, and then he was even able to increase it some. Robbie felt his chest swell up with pride. He was keeping up with his father just fine, and was hardly sweating yet. This wasn't too bad, and he was glad for the switchbacks after all.

About two hours later, Jeff stopped and showed Robbie where they were on the map. He lined up the map with his compass, and then pointed out some areas and specific landmarks on the map that were easy to see. "That's Mount Stewart over there. Can you see how it looks on the map?" The more they looked around at the landmarks and back at the map, the better Robbie was able to understand where everything was. He'd looked at the topographic map before and imagined what the hills looked like, but seeing them here in real life was totally different.

The view from this place was incredible. They were on the side of a mountain, overlooking a long valley. They could see the forested hillside on the other side of the valley, snow-covered mountains in the distance, and they could even see glimpses of the white water that rushed over large boulders in the base of the valley. It looked like a picture from a postcard.

"Wow. This is cool," said Robbie. Then he looked down at his waistline. "I think my stomach just rumbled in agreement. Or… maybe it's rumbling because I'm hungry."

Jeff laughed. "I'm getting hungry, too. Let's eat."

Hundreds of feet below them, the Earth quietly rumbled too.

4. Stealing Lunch

After an hour of "window-shopping", walking around and imagining the riches that waited for him behind every closed door in the neighborhood, Luis' stomach started to growl audibly. Apparently it was time for lunch. He'd only had two cups of bitter, black coffee for breakfast, and now he was coming down from his caffeine buzz, which made him feel irritable.

Although there was food at the halfway-house, lunch was always peanut butter and jelly or tuna fish sandwiches, served with a glass of water or Kool-Aid. As it turned out, the state didn't spend much money on meals for ex-convicts. Once in a while the guy running the place would splurge, and they'd get a can of store-brand soda instead of Kool-Aid, or maybe some cookies, but those things never lasted long. Even though the food was free, Luis was sick of it after the first week. He deserved better than this low-cost slop. A man had rights.

This wouldn't be a problem for long. Luis was a grown man and could take care of himself. He'd get his own lunch today, he decided. He walked two more blocks to the north, to increase the distance between his current residence and his future lunch.

He decided he'd like a roast beef sandwich, a bag of chips, and a can of beer. Unfortunately, he only had two wrinkled dollar bills in his pocket, which wasn't nearly enough. He had no intention of spending his meager cash supply on lunch, anyway. Lunch was a right. He remembered something about rights from a history class he'd taken long ago, in another world, before he'd dropped out of school. The teacher had been blabbering something about the Constitution and its amendments. Then he droned on and on about human rights. Luis' memory wasn't clear, but he thought the right to a free lunch for everyone was in there somewhere.

A minute later, Luis arrived at a gas station convenience store. He'd been there before, and knew they had some decent-looking sandwiches kept cold and fresh in a glass case. He took a baseball cap out of his back pocket and put it on. Then he added a pair of sunglasses, completing his disguise. He was concerned that there would be at least one video camera inside, and he didn't need his picture on the news tonight if something went wrong. That was a lesson he'd learned from his cell-mate, Hank, a thick-headed, tattoo-covered ex-drug-addict (until he got out and could start up again), serving his second sentence for armed robbery after getting caught by a video camera. Luis was no dummy — he wasn't going to get caught like Hank did.

Pretending he was someone who would have no problem paying for anything, he sauntered in and walked up and down the short aisles. He'd shoplifted before, and knew this game. He had started young, with candy bars at a drug store and toys at a Fred Meyer. Later he graduated to taking tools and other supplies from a local Home Depot, which he'd been able to sell to construction workers who were building a new house a few blocks away from where he lived. He'd almost been caught once stealing tools, but the security guard wasn't fast enough. As soon as Luis saw the man walking toward him with a steely look in his eye, he dropped the several wrenches he'd collected and bolted out the door before the man could catch up. He probably would have gotten better at shoplifting if he hadn't been forced to waste several months in jail. There was nothing really worth stealing on the inside, and if you got caught by another inmate, the consequences were worse than going in front of a judge.

He stopped at the sandwich cooler and studied the options. After a minute, with his stomach rumbling even more loudly, he picked out a sandwich. Then he grabbed a bag of tortilla chips from the nearby rack, and was almost ready to go. The attendant, a skinny woman perched behind the register, had been watching him like a hawk from the moment he walked in, but he didn't care. He could outsmart her. He'd wait for the right time and take care of business. He casually walked over to the beer case and watched her reflection in the door glass as he pretended to consider the options. Luis had a plan.

Continuing to stare into the reflection, he noticed a slow-moving, white-haired man approach the register. Perfect. It was time for his next move. Luis opened the door, took out a can of Budweiser, and let the door swing shut on its own. He took another look in the reflection. And as soon as the old man started the laborious process of writing out a check for his gas, Luis ducked out of view of the register, behind a rack of overpriced auto supplies, and slipped the food and the can of beer into his pockets. Then as cool as a cucumber, Luis walked to the door. He pushed it open stepped through. He was almost clear.

"Hey — get back here and pay for that!" the cashier shouted shrilly. He didn't know how she'd seen him, but it didn't matter now. He'd been caught again. Or maybe not. Luis didn't look at the woman. Without a word, he bolted.

Luis pumped his arms and breathed hard as he ran down the street. He'd only been out of prison a couple weeks, and he was already about to get caught committing another crime. He must be a lot rustier than he thought. And maybe the free lunch wasn't such a good idea after all.

The road started to slope downward and Luis increased his speed, running toward the maze of roads that weaved through the neighborhood to the south. He could hear the woman shouting behind him in the distance. She'd actually come out of the store and run a few yards down the street in his direction. Why did he have to get the motivated one?

Then the shouting stopped. He took a quick look back. She was gone, probably to call the police. It could have been worse. By coming out to yell at him, she had given him a head-start.

Although Luis was certainly not the smartest kid in school, or even in his cell block, he had enough street smarts to know that the police would probably start looking for him by driving down this main road, where the woman had seen him last. With that in mind, he took a left onto the next side road.

Panting and already sweating, Luis ran by a woman pushing a baby stroller on the other side of the road. She stopped walking and stared at him. Then she took a cell phone out of her purse and continued to watch him as he passed. He clearly had her attention, and that's the last thing he wanted.

He smiled at her, attempting to look non-threatening, and then slowed to a walk. He figured that the only people who went running around here were doing it for exercise, wearing shorts, sweatshirts and running shoes, not baggy pants and basketball shoes, like he was wearing now. He needed to walk casually if he wanted to blend in. After a minute, he risked a glance back; the woman was walking away and not using her phone, which was good news. He was clear for now. Remembering that he was still wearing the sunglasses and cap, he took them both off and put them back in his pockets.

After walking two more blocks into the heart of the neighborhood, Luis' growling stomach reminded him again that he was still hungry. The recent, unplanned sprinting only added to the hunger. A minute later, he stopped by a thick patch of blackberries growing along the greenbelt that ran through this neighborhood, out of sight of most of the nearby houses, and sat down to eat his lunch. All of that running had made him thirsty. First things first: he popped the top on the can of beer and took a deep drink. After a few large gulps, it was gone, and he was already feeling better. He threw the can into the bushes, unwrapped the sandwich, and took a large bite.

A few minutes later, Luis finished the sandwich and thought about how he could lay low for a while. The cops wouldn't spend much time looking for a shoplifter before they'd find something more important to do. He needed to run out the clock, and he'd be back in business soon. Maybe there was an empty house nearby that he could hide in. Maybe it would even have some cool stuff in it...

5. In the Mountains

Robbie looked at his watch. "12:26. It's definitely lunchtime, and I'm starving. Let's eat those sandwiches that Mom packed." There was something about being outside in the cool mountain air that gave him a king-sized appetite. Of course, the exertion from hiking uphill made him hungry too, but there was something extra-special about hiking and camping and being outside that made him hungry enough to eat a horse.

Jeff and Robbie set their packs against a tree in the small clearing, several feet away from the edge of the overlook. They sat on a fallen tree nearby that served as a bench and would allow them the best view of the valley while they ate. Jeff opened up his pack and removed the two sack lunches. This would be the last fresh food they had to eat for the next three days. After this, they would be eating MRE's[10], freeze-dried backpacking food, trail mix and beef jerky.

Robbie chewed on a bite of his tuna sandwich and felt his energy coming back. It was like playing one of his favorite video games, where the character's health improved as it ate. He finished the sandwich, drank some water, ate some chips, and took out the last part of the lunch, cookies. As he wolfed them down, he knew that they would definitely give him the energy he needed. He was topped off and ready to go.

Jeff was done eating, too. "OK, let's check in with your mother. Are you ready to use your radio on the repeater?"

"You bet. Let's do it." Robbie fished his radio out of his backpack and turned it on. He selected the repeater[11] channel that he had programmed in earlier.

"Hey Dad — this is so cool! If I use a repeater, I'll be able to use this little radio to talk far away! I bet I could even talk to Uncle Joe in Tacoma!"

"You probably could. If you find the right repeater, it will give you dozens of miles of coverage. Repeaters are usually high on a mountain, and will repeat what you transmit to other radios in the whole region." Jeff grabbed a piece of paper and drew a quick sketch of a repeater antenna at the top of a mountain, with people on opposite sides of the mountain talking to each other through the repeater. The first signal went from the man on the left side of the drawing upward to the repeater, and then the signal was re-transmitted downward from the repeater to the second man, on the right side of the drawing, on the other side of the mountain.

"Let's set it up! What's a good repeater to use if we want to talk with Mom when we're up in the mountains camping? You remember we'll be camping next week, right?"

"Yeah, I remember," Jeff said, smiling. *"Let's program that repeater into memory, and add the right tone and offset[12]...*

Robbie pushed the "Talk" button on his radio and said, "This is KE7CTA, calling for KD7KFT, KE7CTA calling for KD7KFT." He waited. There was no reply.

He called again. Nothing. "Do you think she's there?" He looked up at Jeff questioningly.

"KE7CTA, this is KD7KFT. I can hear you clearly. How are you doing?" He did it! His mom could hear him! Robbie grinned from ear to ear with excitement.

Robbie pressed the transmit button again. "We're OK, Mom. The views are awesome up here. And we have a great

31

view of the mountains. We can see Mount Stewart close-up. It's huge. And we just finished eating lunch. Thanks for the sandwiches. They were great."

"You're welcome, sweetheart. I'm glad you liked them."

Jeff had taken his radio out of his pack. "It's time for me to check my radio, too." He turned it on and spoke. "This is NM8J. How was your morning, sweetheart?"

"There's nothing exciting to report here. I'll be taking Lisa to visit her friend later this afternoon, but in the meantime I'll be home, so call again whenever you want. I'll answer."

"OK, good to hear. We're going to get back to our hike soon, just thought we'd check in. Plus, I wanted to make sure that Robbie got some time on the radio, and that we had the right repeater settings programmed in."

"Yep, sounds good. Your signal is clear."

"Oh, one more thing," said Jeff. "Let's see if you can find our location now on the computer map[13]. I'm going to have Robbie transmit our GPS coordinates again using APRS. You should be able to see us north of Cle Elum. I doubt there will be anyone else around to confuse us with. It's not too crowded up here."

"OK, hold on a minute. Let me check the web page. I had it up earlier when Robbie texted me."

Robbie turned a dial and changed the channel to the frequency he had programmed for APRS, 144.390 megahertz, and set the transmission mode so that the radio would automatically send APRS data. As he waited, the radio started transmitting his position.

Marie came back. "I see you! I can see KE7CTA on the map, up in the green area, north and a little bit east of Cle Elum."

Robbie grinned. It was like his mom was a spy, tracking his movements. Neat. And not only that, his radio could be set to two different frequencies at the same time, so even though he was using APRS, he could still monitor on a separate frequency.

Marie called again. "OK, I have to go find Lisa; she's been quiet for too long. Maybe you could transmit your location again tonight when you're in your tent. I'll take another look on the map when it gets dark and see where you decided to camp. I'll see you later. Have fun camping. I love you. "

"It's a date. I love you, too," said Jeff. "NM8J clear." He looked at Robbie. "Don't forget to sign off," he said, as he clipped the radio to his belt.

"Bye Mom, see you soon."

"Bye Robbie, I love you."

"KE7CTA clear."

"KD7KFT clear."

Robbie thought for a second. He probably should have told his mother that he loved her, but it felt weird, saying that in the open airwaves[14] for anyone to hear.

If he only knew what was in store for everyone today, he would have told her more than once.

6. Back in the Game

With food in his belly, Luis turned his attention to finding a place to hole up. Then he froze. A police car had just turned onto his street, three blocks away. Luis was glad it was a regular patrol cruiser, not an undercover car. The light bar on the top made it much easier to spot from a distance. He doubted that the cop had seen him yet, but it was only a matter of seconds before the cop would likely notice him.

He looked left and right, adrenaline pumping through his veins again. He saw a "For Rent" sign hanging on a white wooden post stuck in the front lawn of a house to his right. At first glance, the house looked empty. He didn't have any more time to think about the best place to lay low. The decision had been made for him. Without a second thought, Luis walked up to the house, looking in the front window as he approached. He could see that the large front room had no furniture in it. It was completely bare and obviously unoccupied. This would be a perfect place to hide out. He walked quickly to the left side of the house, where a gated fence blocked the view of the backyard. He opened the gate, stepped through, and closed it behind him. Through a small gap in the wooden slats of the gate, Luis watched the road. He waited. Seconds later, his heart leapt into his throat as the police cruiser slowed down in front of the house and stopped. He saw the cop look at the house, then up and down the street. The officer picked up his radio microphone and said something into it.

A few seconds later, Luis nearly collapsed with relief as the cruiser slowly pulled away, continuing down the road and back toward the convenience store. Luis had been cemented in place, unable to move for fear of the cop seeing some kind of movement through the fence. Now that the danger had passed, he took a deep breath and tried to think clearly again.

Scanning for a way in, he walked around the back side of the house. He was in luck. Some idiot had left the kitchen window open, just a crack, probably to keep the house from smelling musty if a potential renter came by. He pulled out the screen, slid the window open, and pulled himself inside. He scrambled over the kitchen sink and hopped down to the floor. He closed the kitchen window and stood quietly, his heart beating loudly. Breaking into a house was always exciting. He waited quietly for a minute, listening for the sounds of anyone who might be in the house. He didn't hear anything.

Luis walked from room to room, avoiding the empty front room with the big window that faced the street. He didn't want any nosy neighbors seeing him inside. He didn't think anyone saw him walk around to the back of the house, but he didn't want to push his luck.

The house appeared nearly empty until Luis got to the farthest bedroom at the end of the hall. The last renters apparently hadn't finished moving out yet, and had left four cardboard boxes stacked along the wall close to the doorway. They probably planned on coming back to get them, but in the meantime, Luis was going to take a look. He opened the top box — clothes. He pushed it off of the stack, out of the way, spilling the clothes onto the floor. The second box had more clothes. The third box had books. He knocked it to the side too. This sucked. There had to be something good in here.

Determined to get something good out of this break-in, Luis dug into the final box. He pulled out a stack of papers and manila folders and threw them to the side. Then he broke out in a smile as he looked down. Pay-dirt. There was a small stack of green, plastic cases. He immediately recognized them — they were X-Box video games. The cool thing about these games was that he could sell them for cash at the local video game store. He knew this because he'd done it once before, a couple years ago, after he'd pretended to be friends with one of his school-mates and convinced the hapless boy to loan him several games. Luis didn't have an X-Box to play them on, but he did have a plan, and that same day, he walked out of the game store with two crisp, twenty-dollar bills in his pocket, the most money he'd seen in months.

Depending on the games, especially new ones, some stores would pay as much as twenty dollars each, and there were some good ones in this stack. He counted. There were five of them. He stuffed them into the cargo pocket on the side of his pants. They fit perfectly.

Content with his recent good fortune, Luis sat with his back against the wall, opened the bag of chips and ate them slowly, thinking about what else he could find out there in the big world. The games would get him some easy cash, but nowhere near as much as he needed. He'd have to find something else.

Luis was tired after his earlier sprinting, and the adrenaline in his system was wearing off. As he sat on the carpeted floor in the peace and quiet of the nearly-empty bedroom, he started daydreaming about money and freedom. Then he lay down on the floor to relax for a few minutes and pulled some clothes over to use as a pillow. A minute later, he dozed off.

Luis woke with a start and a kink in his neck. He sat up and looked around, then remembered where he was. He looked down at the cheap, plastic digital watch that he'd been forced to buy in order to make sure he got to his lousy job on time. It was 1:00. He hadn't slept long, but he felt a lot better.

Feeling lucky that nobody appeared at the house while he was asleep, he quickly made his way back toward the dining area, then left the easy way, through a sliding glass door that led into the back yard. He walked back the way he'd come, up to the fence with the gate. He looked through the slats and saw no activity anywhere around the front of the house. Without waiting any longer, he opened the gate and made his way to the sidewalk, then continued where he'd left off earlier in the day.

With at least $50 worth of video games in his pocket, Luis was ready for more. His confidence was higher now, and he gave no more thought to whether he was close to home or not. He was back in his element, on top of his game, and ready to make some serious money. Enough of this nickel and dime stuff. Someday he'd hit it big, and he'd have everything he wanted — a nice apartment, a hot car with custom rims, a suitcase full of cash. Women were attracted to a fancy car and a lot of money, so he'd be OK in that department, too. He could order out for pizza or steak sandwiches or whatever else he felt like eating whenever he wanted. And he'd get a nice gun. A shiny one. That would get him by for a while.

Luis was in a relatively well-to-do neighborhood, and he enjoyed guessing which house would have the most valuables in it, which would be the most difficult to break into, and which would be occupied by how many people.

He passed a small, blue, single-story house. It didn't look like a good opportunity. There were no bushes covering the windows. Bushes were handy because he could hide behind them while he tried to force a window open. Also, the front door was clearly visible from the roadway and by neighbors. If the front looked like this, the back door was probably secure, too. This house wasn't worth the risk. Besides, it didn't look like it would have a lot of fancy electronics inside. It just looked like a plain house.

The second house he passed was different. It looked a little fancier. Luis couldn't necessarily say why, but his brain processed the more elaborate curtains, the shiny light fixture above the front door, and most importantly, the new Mercedes parked in the driveway. Nobody bought a Mercedes without also having lots of other valuable stuff. When he gave the house a second look, he could see some side windows from the street, but just barely — they had large, decorative bushes nearby, mostly obscuring the view from where Luis stood. One of these windows could provide a way to get in without being seen. He added up all of these variables and decided that this house would be a good target.

7. Disaster Strikes

Robbie put his radio back into his pack, making sure not to bend the antenna, and zipped it shut.

Jeff walked close to the edge of the overlook and looked over. He pointed downward. "Hey Robbie, look at this. Look how far down this cliff go—"

Everything started to move, all at once. At first Robbie was confused. He thought that his brain must not be processing information correctly. It was like he was on a crazy carnival ride.

What was going on? A millisecond later he figured it out — it was an earthquake! The ground was shaking, and Robbie noticed a noise — a low, deep, loud rumbling that seemed to vibrate in every bone in his body. A second after the quake started, Robbie lost his balance and fell to the ground. It all seemed to happen slowly. The deep, bone-rattling rumbling sound got louder and louder. Small rocks started to fall around him, then larger rocks, all falling down the mountain from the rocky slope that extended hundreds of feet above. Still lying on the ground, Robbie covered his head with his arms and curled up as small as he could, hoping that no rocks would crush him.

The ground kept shaking and rocks continued to rain around him. A fist-sized rock suddenly struck Robbie in the right side of his back, hitting him in the rib. He grunted in surprise and pain and his eyes immediately filled with tears.

"Dad?" Robbie called out, his fear growing. He didn't hear a reply. He called again, louder this time, but he could barely hear his own voice over the thunderous noise.

The few seconds of quaking seemed like an eternity as Robbie lay on the ground, unable to get up, his arms wrapped around his head and his knees curled up into his chest. But as the quake released the last of its pent-up energy, the rumbling gradually decreased, then suddenly stopped. The last of the rocks from the slope above stopped falling, and stillness descended on the mountain[15].

Robbie laid there for several seconds, walking through a mental checklist and moving different parts of his body. Was he all there? Yes, he still had all his parts, and he didn't appear to be bleeding anywhere. He gently prodded his ribs, in front and in back on both sides. His right side was very tender where the rock had struck him, but to his surprise, it wasn't too bad. There would probably be a bruise, but it didn't feel like anything was broken. It certainly could have been worse.

As Robbie shifted his focus outward, his eyes grew wide. Only 15 feet away, he saw a boulder sitting in the clearing, where he had been standing only a few minutes ago. He could have been under that boulder. It was his lucky day.

Or maybe he wasn't so lucky. As Robbie slowly stood up, he looked for his father. Where was he?

Jeff had vanished.

8. A New World

Luis was caught off-guard just like everyone else was when the ground shook. He had a couple seconds to look around and see where all of the loud rumbling sounds were coming from. It didn't take long to realize that they were coming from underneath and all around him. Then he found himself lying on the sidewalk. In his confusion, he tried to get up, but a second later he was lying on the sidewalk again, so he gave up and stayed there for the rest of the quake.

More than once he'd been drinking heavily at a party and unexpectedly found himself on the ground, or he'd woken up somewhere without remembering how he got there. This time he was sober, more alert than usual, but confused nonetheless. As the rumbling slowed down and then finally stopped, he realized what was going on — it was an earthquake.

But the show wasn't over. Many car alarms around the area were blaring and they combined with other, residual crashing sounds to create a raucous symphony that continued long after the earthquake had released its fury. In the midst of the noise, Luis watched in fascination as a power line across the street, already under immense pressure due to a tree that had fallen across it, snapped and fell onto a parked car in a shower of sparks. Although some shrubs nearby had just burst into flame, Luis still viewed it as a win, because that car's alarm stopped and gave his ears some relief. But the decrease in noise didn't last. To his south, a creaking sound that had been slowly growing in volume turned into an outright crash as a rickety carport collapsed into a cloud of dust and debris.

Luis rolled to a sitting position on the sidewalk, not quite ready to stand, and took stock of the situation. This earthquake was obviously a huge one. He started thinking. He didn't think about how to help any people who may be trapped in their houses, or how long cleaning up would take. He didn't think about the effect the earthquake would have on the economy, or wonder how long it would take for the federal government to get involved with relief efforts. He didn't think about any of the pain or suffering that would result from the quake, or how the community could work together to recover from it.

Instead, for whatever reason, the first thing that Luis started to think about was traffic. He thought about cars and trucks stuck in the road, blocked by fallen power-lines, overpasses, trees and buildings. He thought about gridlock. Then his thoughts drifted naturally to one of the topics he thought about most: What would the police be doing? There must be a lot of important problems in the city now, aside from the fact that most of the police officers probably had family locally and would want to make sure they were safe.

It didn't take long for Luis to cleverly conclude that from now on, and at least for a day or two, or maybe even a week, the police were probably not going to show up anywhere quickly, and for certain things, they probably wouldn't show up at all.

He remembered back in his hometown of Detroit, at one of his foster homes, when the police had shown up to investigate a broken window and theft of a television set (which had coincidentally been orchestrated by Luis and two of his trouble-making friends from the neighborhood). Of course there must have been fingerprints and other clues somewhere. But when the police found out the value of the television set was about

$150, one of the investigating officers taught Luis a valuable lesson. As Luis' foster father stood red-faced and scowling in frustration, almost unable to believe what he was hearing, the officer said: "I'm sorry sir, this will be handled by our property crimes bureau, and since the value of the property is below 500 dollars, we'll be putting out an alert to local pawn shops, and that's probably about it. We don't have the resources to do more at this time, so don't hold your breath. I'm sorry."

His foster father had asked, "What about the window? That will probably cost another hundred bucks to fix!"

"That's what insurance is for," the officer had answered.

Then the police drove away and that was the end of it, aside from the fact that Luis had to move to another foster home shortly thereafter. Those foster parents couldn't prove anything, but they had their suspicions. They were kind, but they weren't stupid.

Based on this simple experience, Luis deduced that if the police weren't very concerned about thefts when things were normal, then they would be far less concerned in a situation like this. In only a couple minutes, Luis the high-school dropout deduced something that many local residents never had: the police would not be showing up.

Luis' train of thought kept chugging along. He thought about how some people weren't at home and how they probably wouldn't be home for a long time. Then he thought about the same things he'd been thinking about earlier — the things he wanted that were in those houses. Except now, it should be even easier to get in. Some doors may have sprung open, some windows may already be shattered, and if some more got broken during the rest of the day, would anyone notice?

He started to imagine the jewelry boxes, the coin collections and some of the big scores he'd heard about in prison as he and his buddies small-talked incessantly while playing hundreds of hands of cards over the last two years. Except this was a unique opportunity. Those guys never had it this easy. And Luis knew he probably wouldn't have it this easy ever again. This was it, his big break. As the dust around him settled and the sounds gradually faded, Luis stood up and brushed off his pants, then turned around in a slow circle and surveyed everything he could see. He felt like a kid in a candy store. If he played this right, he could be set for life.

9. At Home

Marie was washing dishes in the sink as Lisa played with her Betsy-Wetsy doll around the corner in the living room, within earshot. Marie thought about Jeff and Robbie, wondering whether they were having fun, and thought about how next year they could all go together. The only camping they had done since Lisa had been born was car-camping, when they'd loaded the truck bed full of supplies, driven to a scenic campground only three hours away, and stayed two nights. It had been a lot of fun, even though she and Jeff hadn't gotten as much sleep as they would have liked.

While car-camping was fun, and the kids enjoyed it, there was a very different feeling to having everything you needed on your back and travelling on foot into an area that was much too rugged for a car or truck to drive. Not only were there fewer people, but there were also no vehicles, making camping in the mountains so... quiet, especially when the kids were asleep. And hiking with their own packs would certainly tire them out.

Marie remembered a trip she had taken with Jeff before they had Robbie. They'd spend three days and two nights in the wilderness, and she'd loved it. The exercise and the fresh air felt fantastic, and she'd had time to just sit, relax and read, with only the sounds of birds chirping in the background. Oh yeah, and the sound of Jeff asking what was for dinner. That was funny. Even though he was more involved in packing the food than she was, for some reason he left it to her to decide what to eat when. Typical man.

Marie placed a dry plate in the cabinet above the counter, and it gave a quiet "clink" as she set it on top of another plate. Clink. Clink.

Marie was confused. All of the dishes were rattling now. Then everything started to rattle.

"Mommy!" Lisa called from the living room. "The house is falling down!"

Marie dropped her towel and ran to the living room as the shaking intensified. She ran to Lisa and picked her up as if she weighed nothing. She darted over to the large, sturdy, wooden table that stood near the exterior wall, pushed Lisa underneath it, and climbed under it with her.

There was no doubt in Marie's mind that this was an earthquake, and a big one. She and Jeff had discussed how to prepare for an earthquake and what to do during one. The Nisqually Earthquake of 2002 was a wake-up call to many including Jeff and Marie, who had lived in Seattle at the time. A lot of educational information had been published about the fact that Seattle and Bellevue were built on top of a fault line (coincidentally named the Seattle Fault) that ran east to west, and the local government had made efforts to educate the public on the possible dangers of a far larger earthquake, how to prepare for it, and what to do if it occurred.

Marie knew that the first thing she needed to do was get herself and Lisa somewhere safe, and in this area of the house, the safest location was under this sturdy table near the intersection of two load-bearing walls (walls designed to bear weight). Well, it was safest as long as the house didn't collapse completely, but she didn't see a point in thinking about that now.

Lisa cried out as the shaking continued. "Mommy, the house is going to break!"

"No, it won't, baby. The ground is shaking a little bit, but we'll be OK," Marie said loudly, to make sure Lisa could hear her over the noise. "Just stay here with me until it's done."

Lisa continued to cry, terrified, as Marie held her in her arms and rocked her, shushing reassuringly.

Though it seemed like an eternity, the shaking stopped after about fifty seconds. The house continued to creak, and they could hear crashing sounds from inside and out, as things continued to settle, some falling and breaking, some sliding or tipping, gravity eventually pulling them to the lowest point they could reach. Gradually, the noise died down, with the exception of car alarms that continued to wail and honk, as if protesting the damage that had been done.

Marie and Lisa were still huddled under the table, unharmed.

"Are we safe, Mommy?"

"I don't know if we are yet," Marie replied. "The ground may move a little bit more, which happens sometimes. Let's just sit a little bit longer to make sure."

They sat under the table, holding onto each other, wondering if the worst of it was over. Eventually the car alarm noise died down, the earth remained still, and the neighborhood grew quiet.

10. Taking Stock

"Dad! Where are you?" Robbie yelled, feeling the fear well up in his chest. His father was gone. He spun around frantically as he looked. There was no sign of his father. He spun around again. He must have missed him. He could be lying down near that log, or over by that rock. He looked again. Nothing.

"Dad!" he called again. There was no reply. In fact, there was no sound whatsoever. No birds were chirping, and the breeze that had cooled them earlier in the day was now gone. After all the noise of the earthquake, the silence almost seemed unreal. Adding to the unreal feeling, which was starting to feel downright nightmarish, his father had apparently disappeared off the face of the earth.

Robbie sat on the ground, dumbfounded, confused and scared. He had to stop and think for a minute. He could hardly believe what had happened. It was a freaking *earthquake*. This was crazy, like being in a disaster movie. This stuff never happened in real life, and he'd never come close to experiencing anything like it. He'd done a book report about earthquakes in school, but he never thought he'd actually be in one. He thought back to what he had read about. Earthquakes usually caused much more damage in cities, where there are taller buildings, more bridges, lots of glass that can break and bricks that can fall, power lines that can fall down, and… his mother and sister. They were back in Bellevue, all alone! Were they OK? It seemed like the situation was getting worse and worse. And where was his father?

While he was still collecting his wits and slowing down his racing mind, he heard a voice. It was faint, as if far away.

"Robbie…"

It was his dad! It sounded like he was far away, but that would be impossible. He was just here a few second ago. Where was it coming from? He stood up and looked around again. He was still alone, and he couldn't tell what direction the voice was coming from.

"Robbie…"

"Dad! I'm here!" he called back, trying to keep the fear out of his voice, "Where are you?"

"Robbie — I'm down here."

Robbie looked around again and remembered where his father had been standing just before the earthquake hit. He was over by the edge of the cliff. The *tall* cliff.

"Dad?" Robbie called back, as he walked slowly toward the edge.

"I'm down here — be careful" Jeff called back. "Don't fall over."

Now Robbie could tell where the sound was coming from. Robbie got on all fours and crawled toward the edge, then peered over. And there was his father, about 12 feet down, on a ledge that was about six feet wide and eight feet long. It was just long enough for an adult to lie down. Below the ledge there was nothing but sheer cliff that descended another 90 feet. And on both sides of the ledge, the cliff wall was smooth. Jeff was trapped.

"Dad! Are you OK?" Robbie said as he looked over the edge. He could feel tears welling in his eyes, but he wanted to stay strong — his father needed him. But as much as he tried to hold it back, a tear escaped and ran down his face as he looked down anxiously. He was afraid.

"I'm OK, mostly," Jeff said. "I slipped over while the ground was shaking. And I'm lucky that I landed here, or I'd probably be…" He didn't need to finish the sentence. The sharp rocks at the base of the cliff finished it for him.

"I think I may have broken my ankle, and my arm is bleeding."

He cautiously tried to get up, put a small amount of weight on his right foot, and gasped in pain. He quickly sat back down and closed his eyes tightly, breathing hard between his clenched teeth.

"Yeah, my ankle really hurts, and I don't know how I'm going to get up over the ledge. I'm stuck."

This was bad. Robbie had never heard his dad talk like this. He heard the worry, the pain and fear in Jeff's voice, and it scared him. "Is there any way you can climb up?" Robbie asked.

"The side of the cliff here only has a couple of spots that look like they could hold my weight. And even if I thought I could climb up, one false move with this bad ankle, and I'd probably fall all the way down this time. I'm not sure I'd try it even if my ankle wasn't hurt. I don't want to tempt fate and risk falling again. I was lucky enough this time." Jeff was almost talking to himself now, obviously thinking about what to do next.

"So what do we do?" Robbie asked, trying to keep the tears contained.

"Let's just think about it for a minute. And while I think about it, is everything safe up there? Is there any danger of a rockslide, or are there any trees that may be ready to fall now? Go check right away. I don't want something happening to you." He grimaced as the pain hit him again.

Robbie collected his wits and scanned the hillside behind him, trying to be methodical about it so he didn't miss anything. He looked up the slope from where the rocks had slid down. Nothing was moving, and the dust had settled. It didn't seem like any trees were leaning unusually.

"I think it's safe up here, Dad. But what about you?"

"Can you see our packs up there?"

Robbie looked back at the center of the clearing. He saw his backpack, yellow and blue, lying flat now, next to where he had propped it up. But his dad's pack wasn't where he'd left it. He looked closer, and walked up to the tree that his pack had been leaning against. A small section of earth had torn away from the cliff face, and apparently taken his dad's backpack with it.

"Bad news, Dad. Your pack is gone."

"Are you sure? Look again. Maybe it tipped over behind a rock or something."

Robbie knew it was gone, but walked back and looked again anyway.

"It's still gone, Dad."

Jeff sighed. "OK, then we'll make the best of this. Get me your first aid kit. I have to stop this bleeding."

Robbie looked at his father's arm more closely. There was a lot of blood on the lower left arm, where he must have gouged it on a rock as he fell.

Robbie stepped back and walked over to his pack. It looked undamaged. He quickly opened it and pulled out the first aid kit, which was packed near the top. It was a smaller-sized kit, made by Adventure Medical, and it was full of useful supplies. To make it even more useful, Jeff had added some supplies of his own. Since he had volunteered at a local fire department as an emergency medical technician earlier in his life, he was familiar with some medical supplies that weren't in every first aid kit, and made sure to include them on his own.

Robbie crawled back to the edge and called down, "I have it Dad, but how do I get it down to you? Do you want me to drop it down?"

"No — I don't want to risk dropping it and losing it. Get some 550 cord[16] from your pack, tie it on, and lower it to me."

Robbie went back to his pack and fished around until he found the coil of cord. It was strong enough to hold Jeff's weight; the "550" indicated that it could hold 550 pounds of weight. However, it was too thin to hold onto without slipping. Robbie quickly tied one end to a loop in the side of the kit and lowered it down to his dad.

"Thanks Robbie," Jeff said, as he opened up the kit. He pulled out a small packet, about twice the size of a tea bag, and set it aside. Then he pulled out another plastic package, about the size of a rolled-up sock. He tore the end off of it, pulled out a tightly-rolled bandage, opened it up partially, and set it on his lap with the sterile white pad side facing up. Then he pulled back the torn part of the arm of his shirt, exposing the wound on his lower arm. The bleeding had slowed, but dark-colored blood was still leaking continuously. That was good news, if you could call it good. Since the blood was dark red, indicating that it didn't contain much oxygen, he had injured a vein, not an artery, which would have probably been spurting bright-red, oxygen-rich blood. This bleeding should be easier to stop. Jeff pulled out a piece of gauze, wiped away some of the blood that was still flowing, and set the gauze to the side[17].

Jeff picked up the small foil packet and tore the top off. Then he poured the contents, which looked like sea salt, directly into the bloody wound.

"What's that stuff, Dad?" Robbie asked.

"These are Celox granules," Jeff said. "This stuff causes clotting super-quickly. I need to get this bleeding stopped now. I need to keep as much blood inside me as possible." He didn't need to say the last part, but he felt better talking about what he was doing. It helped him focus.

Seconds later, Jeff's bleeding had already slowed, as the granules reacted with the blood to form a stable, solid blood clot, preventing any further loss of blood from the wound. Then Jeff picked up the bandage that had been sitting in his lap and placed the sterile, white side down on the wound. He wrapped the long, green end around his arm once, then slipped it through small plastic clip, and then back around the other way. Then he wrapped and wrapped until he reached the end, which he secured with a separate plastic clip.

"That should do it," Jeff said, as he very gently moved his arm around, making sure it was relatively comfortable. "These trauma bandages are pretty easy to use. I'm glad I added one to your kit." Then he pulled something else from the kit. It looked like a flattened, orange snake, coiled into a cylinder. It was a rolled up SAM splint[18], made out of thick, moldable aluminum foil, and covered by thin, dense foam. He set it in his lap and gingerly removed his right shoe, exposing the ankle. He took off the sock and looked at the ankle. It was swollen to almost twice its normal size, especially around the upper ankle area. He gently touched around the top, the sides, and the bottom of his foot.

"This may be good news," Jeff said, as he gently pushed and squeezed different locations on and above his foot, wincing when he touched the more tender spots.

"Are you serious, Dad? That looks painful, and you just fell over a cliff! How could this be good news?"

"My ankle probably isn't broken. I sprained it before, when I was young, and it was pretty much like it is now. I bet that I sprained it again. It's hard to tell, but I'm going to think positively. Yes, it's just sprained, I think."

"OK, now what?" Robbie asked.

"I'm going to splint my ankle so that I don't damage it more by moving any injured parts around.

"I wish I could help, Dad."

"You'll be able to help in a minute. Let me finish this and clear my head."

Jeff put his sock back on, then took the splint, unrolled it, and folded it into a "U" shape, with his heel in the bottom, and the sides coming up around both sides of his ankle and extending up to his calf. This would help keep his ankle stable. He took out two small pieces of cloth (called "cravats") from the bag, and used them to tie the splint at the top to his leg, and at the bottom, around the top and bottom of his foot, but not over the swollen area of his ankle. When this was done, he reached down and pinched his big toe, looking at the color of the toenail. The color under the nail turned white as he pressed, and then turned pink again as he released the pressure, indicating that it was getting enough circulation. Then he unlaced his hiking boot all the way down, opened it up, and slowly, gently slipped it over his foot. It fit, but just barely. He pulled the slack out of the laces and tied the boot at the top.

"Keeping my boot on may help keep some of the swelling down. And if I don't put it back on now, I may not be able to fit it on later. I'll check on my foot regularly to make sure it's still getting enough circulation." He fished around further in the first aid kit, found a small packet of ibuprofen, opened it, and popped the pills into his mouth[19].

"This should help a little with the swelling." Jeff took a deep breath and exhaled slowly. Then he took another, and exhaled again. He was calming down. "OK, what's next? Let's see if our radios are OK. Is yours still working?"

Robbie scooted back from where he had been laying near the cliff edge, opened up his pack, took out the handheld radio, and pressed the power button. It turned on as he expected. He went back to the edge.

"Mine still works. But where is yours? Wasn't it in your pack?"

"I clipped it to my belt after we talked to your mom. And thank God it didn't fall off. It's dirty and scratched, but the antenna isn't broken and I just checked it — it powers up OK. Turn back to our primary frequency and call me."

Robbie changed frequencies and transmitted. Jeff could hear it fine. Then he called Robbie back, to verify he was also transmitting fine. No problems.

"OK, I have a plan," Jeff said. "Here's the quick version. I'm going to wait here, because there's nothing else I can do. And you're going to get me out of this."

"Uh... OK."

"OK, I want you to lower some stuff to me. I'm getting cold. The last thing I need is to get hypothermia, and this ledge is pretty exposed, so I'll need your sleeping bag, sleeping pad, and emergency survival blanket — that will keep me from getting too cold. Pull up the cord and tie it to the bag. Make sure the survival blanket is inside the bag. Please be very careful, and try to keep back from the edge. The ground might be unstable because of the quake."

Robbie pulled out his sleeping bag, loosened the drawstring on the bag that contained it, and slipped in the Mylar survival blanket. He tied the cord to the sleeping bag, wrapped it around the sleeping pad and tied another knot, then carefully lowered the bag and pad over the edge.

11. Rescue Plan

"I have it. Hold on a minute." Jeff had the sleeping bag and pad with him on the ledge now, and was untying the cord that Robbie had used to lower it.

Robbie waited for a half minute.

"OK, you can pull it back up. All yours."

Robbie inched forward and poked his head over the edge. His father sat there, unfolding the sleeping mat and pulling the sleeping bag out of its sack.

"OK, I'm going to try calling for help. The Search and Rescue people should have no problem getting me out of here safely." Jeff turned on his radio and called: "This is NM8J with emergency traffic — can anyone hear me?" He heard nothing. This was a problem. He tried again. Nothing.

"I have bad news, Robbie. Do you remember the 'beep-beep' that we'd hear on the repeater when we would transmit? Well, my radio is fine, but I don't hear that beep. That means that the repeater isn't working as it should. Something was probably damaged in the earthquake. Repeaters often have backup power supply, but I don't know if they're meant to survive an earthquake like that one. Just in case, try with your radio too — channel five."

Robbie changed to memory location number five in his frequency list. He transmitted: "Can anybody hear me?"

No beep-beep. No answer. Nothing.

"Now what, Dad?" Robbie could feel his stomach tightening up. If they couldn't reach the outside world, and his father was trapped below and couldn't climb up, what could they do? Robbie couldn't pull up his father on his own. He didn't know how to drive, even if he could get back to the truck. Would his father die of hypothermia, exposed on the rock face? What could they do?

"Don't worry, son." His father's words were full of confidence, and they made Robbie feel better. "You'll hike back to the truck, get some rope, bring it back, and I'll be able to climb up."

Just then, they were both surprised to hear their radios simultaneously announce:

"This is a NOAA[20] alert. There are reports of an earthquake with the epicenter near the Seattle metropolitan area. Initial measurements indicate that the earthquake is 7.6 on the Richter scale. It was felt north of Vancouver, British Columbia, and as far south as Eugene, Oregon. Wide-scale power outages have been reported. Most phone lines and cell towers are not functional at this time. More information will follow shortly. In the meantime, please do not attempt to use your cell phone unless you have a life-threatening emergency. Emergency services are limited at this time."

With a jolt, Robbie remembered his mother and sister at home. "Dad! What about Mom and Lisa? Do you think they're OK?"

"Don't worry, Robbie. They were most likely still at home. And since we had our house earthquake retrofitted, they should be safe."

Three years before, Marie and Jeff had endured two long weekends of workers crawling around under their house, drilling, nailing, and hammering as they made a variety of modifications to ensure that the wooden house structure was firmly secured to the concrete foundation. Their house had been built in the 40s, long before the building code was updated with higher standards for earthquake safety. Additional hardware and effort was required to make sure that the house didn't simply slide right off of its foundation if an earthquake happened. Jeff and Marie also made many other simple modifications on their own, for example, securing the water heater to the walls with metal straps and securing tall shelves to the walls.

"Also, Mom knows where the gas shutoff is, and we have plenty of batteries and extra fuel for the generator. They'll be OK."

But Jeff knew there was no way to tell whether they were safe. And since there was no way to know, there was no use worrying about it, and he didn't want to upset Robbie. They had to focus on getting home, then they could worry about whatever else needed fixing.

"OK Robbie — here's the plan. You hike back to the truck and get the rope. Then we'll hopefully find a way to get me back up this cliff and we'll go from there. Do you remember how to get back to the truck?"

"Um…" Robbie didn't remember.

12. Inspecting the Damage

"Lisa, I'm going to get out and see if the house is all right. You stay right there, OK? I want to make sure it's safe, and for now, you are probably in the safest place. Wait for Mommy."

Lisa nodded quietly. Marie looked around quickly, then grabbed a teddy bear that had been sitting on a nearby chair.

"You keep Teddy safe now. He'll be with you while I look around."

Lisa nodded again, distracted by the new responsibility of keeping her teddy bear safe.

Marie quickly walked around the house. Initially, it appeared to be in good shape. One window was cracked from top to bottom in the dining room area, and several books had fallen from their shelves. But since the shelves had been secured to the walls, they were all thankfully still upright. She looked quickly through the kitchen — only one dish that had been sitting on the counter appeared to have fallen, and its pieces lay all over the floor. More good luck, thought Marie, I never did much like the design on that dish. So far, so good.

"Is everything OK in there?" she asked Lisa.

"Yeah. Teddy is worried, but I'm taking good care of him," Lisa replied, with a confidence that filled Marie with pride. Her little girl was already showing an internal strength that would make her into a fine woman someday, as long as Marie could keep her safe long enough…

"Good job, baby. Keep up the good work. I'm going to keep looking around. Stay where you are."

"OK, Mommy."

Marie walked slowly up the stairs, making sure they were stable and that everything was still more or less level. Though the stairs looked the same, and they felt stable, the creak she'd grown used to on the second step was gone now. And when she reached the middle landing, she heard a new squeak. The house had adjusted itself during the quake, but still seemed OK.

Once she'd climbed the stairs, Marie took stock of the bedrooms and two bathrooms. Boxes had fallen off of the shelf in the guest bedroom and Jeff's office was a mess, but it was always a mess. He may not even notice what had changed, she thought to herself in amusement. All in all, the house appeared to have weathered the earthquake intact.

Then Marie stopped in her tracks. She remembered something, one of the most dangerous things that could happen in an earthquake. She turned and ran down the stairs as fast as she could.

Marie remembered a discussion that had taken place in the CERT (Community Emergency Response Team)[21] training she'd taken with Jeff last year. The instructor had explained that one of many potential dangers during or after an earthquake is a natural gas leak and a possible explosion or fire that could result from it. They made it clear that one of the first things people should do right after a quake is to make sure they don't have a natural gas leak, and if there is any suspicion of a leak, shut the gas off immediately[22].

When she reached the bottom of the stairs, she turned right and continued hastily to the garage. Wading through a stack of boxes and other junk that had fallen over, she made her way to the door that led to the back patio and walked outside.

Marie quickly walked around the back of the garage, wondering what she'd fine. As the turned the corner, she realized that she was right to be concerned. She didn't have to get close to realized that the squatting gas meter was hissing at her menacingly.

Marie's eyes widened. There was obviously a leak, and hopefully it was on the side of the meter that she could control. Otherwise, they might need to evacuate the house until either the gas company released the pressure in the lines or fixed the leak somehow. And considering what had just happened, Marie didn't think she would be getting quick service from the gas company for a long time to come.

Marie ran back to the garage. Just inside the doorway, she saw the special wrench hanging on the wall in the same place it had hung, unused, for years. Marie snatched the wrench and went back to the meter.

Marie could smell the thick odor of the gas in the air. Since the natural gas producers added a smelly, sulfur-like substance to the natural gas, which would otherwise be odorless, anyone could tell that gas was leaking, even if the hissing sound didn't give it away. The smell reminded her to work quickly. She couldn't afford to be overcome by the gas if she breathed too much of it.

Before Marie got all the way back to the meter, she took a deep breath of uncontaminated air, held it, and darted forward. She fitted the rectangular opening in the wrench to the valve on the meter, then carefully but firmly pushed. It didn't budge. She pushed again, with nearly all of her strength this time. Even though she'd just taken a deep breath, she could feel a burning sensation in her lungs as she began to use up her small supply of oxygen. She pushed harder, and the valve suddenly gave way, nearly sending Marie sprawling as she momentarily lost her balance. She was running out of breath at this point, and could feel her diaphragm clenching as it involuntarily tried to pull in the contaminated air in its search for more oxygen. But she didn't want to take the time — she needed to get this job done now, before the gas spread further. Now that the valve could move without much difficulty, she finished pushing it through its range of motion and closed it completely. The hissing stopped. The gas was contained. With the last of the clean air remaining in her lungs, she ran the several yards back around the corner of the garage and stopped, gasping as she recovered.

Marie moved back into the garage, breathing deeply and trying to clear her head well enough to decide what to do next[23]. She needed to check further, to make sure the house was safe. She walked back into the house and checked on Lisa.

"Stay where you are, baby. Everything is OK, but I need you to stay there and keep looking after Teddy."

"He's doing OK now, Mommy."

Marie walked out the door, into the front yard, and then she turned back toward the house and looked up and down the facade, looking for any cracks, obvious damage, fallen trees that were resting on the roof, collapsed power lines, or anything else dangerous. She continued her survey around the house, which only took a couple more minutes. Then she looked outward, to see if any neighbors were in immediate danger, whether any structures were on fire, or if there was anything else life-threatening to her and Lisa, or to her neighbors.

From the slightly elevated vantage point in the yard, she didn't see any collapsed houses, which was great news. Unfortunately, two carports had collapsed, one across the street and one next door, but the main house structures seemed to be intact.

Confident that there was no imminent danger, Marie walked back into the house to give Lisa the "all clear" and decide what to do next.

13. Get Rope

It was a good thing Jeff had taken time to show Robbie where they were on the map and where they were going. Even though Robbie didn't know how to get back from memory alone, he knew he could figure it out. And since he had a map and compass, he could make sure he was on the right path. It shouldn't be very complicated. At least, he hoped it wouldn't be. He needed to show his dad that he could do this. Besides, he didn't really have a choice. Both their lives hung in the balance.

"I can use the map, Dad. I can do it."

"Good," Jeff replied. He reached into his pocket. "Here are the keys — lower the cord again. I'll tie them on. I'm afraid to throw them up. If I miss, we'd be in even hotter water…"

Robbie lowered the cord, Jeff tied the keys on, and Robbie pulled them up. He put them in his backpack.

"Inside the truck, in the extended cab, behind the passenger seat on the floor, there's a coil of rope. That should work fine, as long as we can find something to tie it to up there. How quickly do you think you can make it down and back?"

"It took us about an hour to hike up here, and that was uphill. Downhill should be faster, and I have plenty of energy left, maybe 30 minutes down, and another hour to come back. It looks like an hour and a half total."

Robbie started to put on his pack, and then a thought came to him. "Why should I take everything in my backpack? I bet it will be faster with less stuff."

"Good thinking Robbie. You're a smart boy!"

"I'm not a boy!" Sometimes it bugged him when his dad called him a boy. It wasn't a big deal when he was younger, but now he was 14 years old, after all. Teenagers weren't boys any more, he thought.

"You're a smart *young man*," Jeff replied patiently. "Yes, you should take non-essential stuff out of your pack."

Robbie dumped out his backpack. He moved items into two piles: one pile to take and one pile to leave behind. He took a survival kit, flashlight, rain jacket, radio with spare batteries[24], his Leatherman multi-tool, a Clif Bar, a bottle of water, and some other essentials. And the truck keys, of course. He left behind extra clothing, extra food, his water filter, stove, stove fuel canisters, and some other gear. His pack was much lighter.

"OK dad. My pack's a lot lighter now. This will definitely help me go faster."

"Great. Any questions before you go?"

Robbie thought for a few seconds. "No."

"OK, go get that rope and get me out of here!"

"I'll do a radio check about half-way, and I'll radio you again when I'm at the truck. Do you think we'll be able to hear each other at this distance?"

"Yes, talking at this range should be no problem. You can leave your radio on if you want, just in case. If we're not transmitting or receiving often, it won't drain the batteries quickly. I'll talk to you soon."

Robbie turned his radio on, clipped it to the backpack waist-belt, and started trotting down the trail.

After a few minutes, he increased his speed. The trail and its surrounding still looked familiar, and most of the time the trail wasn't very rough. He noticed that his heart was pounding harder now, and he wasn't sure if it was because he was moving quickly, because he was scared for his dad, because he was scared for his mom and sister, or because he was scared in general. He didn't care. He had to focus on getting back to the truck as soon as possible.

As Robbie jogged down another straight stretch on a switchback, he came to a fork in the trail. It looked familiar and he jogged right on through, taking the left path. He passed two more forks in the trail as he kept jogging, and took the second one, this time to the right.

A few minutes later, as he rounded a bend, he saw a clearing with a creek running by on the far side, and slowed to a walk, breathing heavily. It looked like a great place to camp. But there was a problem. They hadn't passed this clearing on the way up. They hadn't crossed a creek, or even walked near a creek that he could remember. And Jeff would have definitely pointed out a creek if one had been nearby. With a sinking feeling in the pit of his stomach, Robbie realized that he had made at least one wrong turn. He was lost.

14. Lost!

"What is the first thing you are supposed to do when you get lost in the woods?" Robbie asked himself. His father's words from a previous hiking trip, when they'd realized that they had taken a wrong turn, echoed in his ears. "Stop moving and figure out where you are. Take a minute to use your brain, the most valuable tool you have..." But his dad wasn't there to help him reason through the problem now. He was waiting on the side of a cliff! Robbie needed to keep going. But if he continued without knowing where he was, he could get even more lost.

Robbie stopped running and wiped the sweat off his forehead. He breathed heavily and leaned forward with his hands on his thighs, trying to force more air into his lungs. He had to get to the truck, and this stupid mistake had cost him precious time.

In the back of his mind, a doubt surfaced. Would he be able to save his father's life? Had his mistake caused a delay that would somehow put his father in more danger? And what about his mother and sister?

Robbie shook his head and dismissed the doubt. He couldn't stop, and definitely couldn't give up. Everything would be OK. His mother and sister were probably fine, and his father would be out of danger soon. But he had to find his way back to the truck.

He walked over to a fallen log, sat down, pulled out his water bottle, and gulped down a mouthful. Then his stomach jumped into his throat — did he bring a map and compass? He opened his pack in a near panic, yanked out his jacket so he could see better and there they were. They were two of the first things he packed. He breathed a sigh of relief, then unfolded the map and set down the compass, making sure it wasn't near his radio or anything else metal.

"Where does the red part of the compass needle point, Robbie?"

"North, Dad."

"Are you sure?"

"Yes, that's what you told me. Plus, I read it in the instructions."

"Watch this." Jeff took the compass and walked over to the oven. And as he held it close to the oven door, the needle swung wildly in the opposite direction!

It had been pointing east, and now it pointed west.

"What's going on, Dad?"

"The needle is magnetic, and usually it's only affected by the Earth's magnetic field. But if you put it near something with iron in it, it will be more attracted to that, and it'll move in that direction. The stove has some steel in it, so if you get the compass too close to the stove, it's more attracted to the metal in the stove than it is to the North Pole. So guess what you have to make sure of whenever you use a compass?"

"Keep it away from metal, so the needle points in the right direction."

Jeff smiled at him. "Smart boy!"

Robbie saw that north was back the way he had come. But not quite north — it was slightly northwest. Then he looked at the map. "Start with what you know," he told himself. He found where they started, where the truck was parked. He followed the trail upward to where they had stopped before the earthquake. He looked at it for a minute, thinking. He looked up and down the map, along the trail they had hiked on earlier. But where was he now? He followed the trail back downward, looking for the fork in the trail that he had taken. It must have been the wrong direction. But there were apparently several forks in this trail, and they were all near the area where he thought he had turned. He still wasn't sure where he was, or how he would get back. He could feel fear growing heavier and heavier. He took three deep, cleansing breaths in an attempt to clear it away.

Wait a second, he thought. The creek — it had to be on the map, too. He looked at the map again, scanning for the thin blue line that would indicate a creek. And there it was. And he could see that trails came right up to the creek in two different places. One spot on the map was about two inches away to the west. Robbie double-checked the map legend. An inch was one mile, and there was no way he'd travelled two miles in the wrong direction in just the last twenty minutes; he wasn't walking that quickly. His location must be the other place where the creek bumped up against the trail.

He followed that trail upward and intersected with the main trail they had taken up earlier. That was the place he took the wrong turn. Now he knew where he was, and he sighed in relief. Robbie took another deep breath to calm himself and took another swig of water. He folded up the map with the path showing on the top and started walking briskly, back the way he had just come.

It only took a few minutes for Robbie to backtrack to the point where he'd taken the wrong turn. He was flooded with relief when he reached the original trail again. Now he was one hundred percent sure that he was on the right path. As he relaxed slightly, he suddenly realized that in his confusion he had forgotten to update his father!

He thought about his father sitting alone, trapped on a ledge, waiting for help, maybe even scared... Robbie quickly grabbed his radio and called "NM8J, this is KE7CTA, can you hear me?"

"KE7CTA this is NM8J. I can hear you clearly. Is everything OK? I was getting ready to call you. Do you have the rope yet?"

"Umm... I'm OK. I don't have the rope yet."

"What's wrong. Are you OK?" Jeff could obviously tell that something wasn't right. Robbie could hear the concern in his voice.

"Yeah. I took a wrong turn, but I figured out where I am now. It shouldn't slow us down much." He felt embarrassed — he should have paid more attention on the way down. His dad was depending on him and he was screwing it up. How could he be so stupid in such an important situation? Shaking his head to himself, he started down the trail again with the radio in his hand.

Jeff replied "That's good to hear. Good job keeping a level head and getting un-lost. Just let me know when you get back down. See if anyone else or any other vehicles are down there. If there are any other vehicles, see if you can find some paper in the truck and leave a note for someone, including my location, and tell them what happened. Let them know I'm injured. Maybe we'll get lucky and get some help."

"OK, Dad. I'm going now."

"See you soon."

Robbie continued down the trail. Since he was now on the main trail, it was a simple route back. He passed another fork in the trail, but this time he double-checked the map and compass, and was sure he was going the right way. He could tell he was getting closer when he saw a cluster of boulders on the side of

Andrew Baze

the trail that he had seen earlier that day, right after they'd started up the mountain. He rounded the bend and there was the truck, sitting alone in the parking lot. It sat there like a loyal dog, waiting for his master. There were no other vehicles parked in the area. Robbie remembered that two vehicles were parked there when they had arrived earlier, but they had obviously left already, probably trying to get home. And there was no cliff nearby they could have fallen off of, Robbie thought wryly. He and his father were really on their own now.

Robbie was so excited and relieved to see their truck that he ran the last few yards to the truck. He dropped his pack and fished around for the keys. He found them right away and opened the driver side door. He unlocked all the doors, and then opened the rear door. He quickly scanned for the coil of rope Jeff had mentioned earlier. He didn't see it. Where was it? It had to be there. If it wasn't there, they would have a whole new set of problems, and they didn't need any more problems!

Robbie remembered what his father had said, and smacked his hand to his forehead. The rope was behind the passenger seat, not the driver seat. He ran around the back of the truck and opened the back door on the passenger side. He still didn't see the rope. Then Robbie moved a folded tarp that was lying across some gear on the floor. The rope was there, coiled up and ready for adventure. "Mission accomplished!" Robbie told himself. Well, this little part of the mission anyway. He quickly stuffed the rope into his backpack and looked around for anything else that he may need. He didn't need road flares or a tarp or a toolkit, and nothing else looked that important, so he closed the doors, locked the truck, and made another call on his radio.

"NM8J this is KE7CTA."

"KE7CTA, this is NM8J. Do you have the rope?"

"Yes, I have the rope and I'm headed back. Can you think of anything else we might need from the truck?"

"No. That's all we need. I'll see you soon. NM8J monitoring."

"KE7CTA monitoring[25]," Robbie replied, as he started one more trek up the mountain.

15. Water

Earlier in the day, Marie flipped a light switch as she entered the garage, on her way to turn off the gas. In the back of her mind, she noticed the light hadn't turned on, but didn't have time to think about it. Now she had time to think, and she realized that the power was off. No lights, no furnace fan, no refrigerator motor, no TV. She'd have to do some things differently[26].

She thought about the food in the refrigerator and the freezer; some of it would last through the next day, if she didn't open the refrigerator often. The food in the freezer would quickly thaw and spoil if she didn't come up with a plan to keep it cool. She remembered that their next door neighbor had put a new chest freezer in his garage last summer, and he had let her use some of the space when they both pooled their funds to purchase a side of beef. The freezer had been packed fully then, and the last time she'd gone over to retrieve a half dozen steaks, she saw he was keeping it relatively full. Now, even with the power out, since the freezer was very well insulated, the food would probably stay frozen for at least a few days. Maybe she would be able to move some frozen food from her less efficient freezer into his, if there was room. This was a problem she'd think about later. She had bigger fish to fry. For example, what were they going to drink?

When Marie had taken the CERT course they had covered a variety of topics, from first aid to search and rescue to putting out fires. And in the part of the course where they discussed disasters, the instructors had put extra focus on earthquakes, since one of those was much more likely to happen in their area, versus a hurricane or tornado. After discussing various scenarios in training, Marie wasn't actually surprised to learn that the power was out or that the gas was leaking.

Marie went to the sink and washed her hands. As she was drying her hands, she stopped, surprised. The water was still flowing!

"Why would that work?" she wondered out loud as she finished drying. Everything else had failed — why didn't the water stop flowing, too? Thinking quickly, she decided that she wasn't going to look a gift horse in the mouth. Based on what she learned in her training about what would happen to city utilities during or after a quake, she didn't expect the water pressure to last. She went to the kitchen and started pulling pots and pans from the cupboards.

"Lisa, it's time to get to work. Come on out here."

Lisa was tired of consoling Teddy and scampered into the kitchen.

"I have a very important job for you. We may run out of water soon and we need to save some for later. Please start filling up these pots with water, and don't spill. We may not get more anytime soon."

"OK, Mommy."

"Good. Make sure he stays safe and doesn't get scared."

Marie found a step-stool and positioned it in front of the sink. Lisa climbed it and started filling some of the smaller pans.

Marie went back up the stairs to the master bathroom. She shook her head and smiled to herself as she climbed the stairs, knowing that Jeff was going to have something smug to say to her about what she was about to do. She walked into the bathroom and kneeled down in front of their claw-foot tub. She reached underneath and pulled. With a tearing sound, the masking tape holding the package to the bottom of the tub gave way, and she withdrew a plastic-wrapped, rectangular object.

In minutes, Marie had opened the package, unfolded a heavy-duty, flexible plastic container which was nearly as large as the tub, and placed it into the tub. She then attached a plastic hose that stuck out of the container to the faucet, and turned it on. The plastic container slowly started to fill.

Earlier that year, Jeff had grinned as he opened a package that Marie had picked up at the post office that day. He'd gone online and purchased a special container called a "WaterBOB". It was a large, thick plastic bag designed to sit in a bathtub and store water in emergencies. This one would hold about 100 gallons of water. It came with a hose for filling, and a special pump for removing water. Aside from the fill tube and the pump for extracting the water, it kept the water completely enclosed, effectively keeping out air, dust, bacteria and other debris. Marie never expected they'd need to use it, and occasionally made fun of Jeff's purchase. If she had to eat her words, at least she'd be able to wash the words down with clean, safe water, she thought to herself with a smile.

As the bag in the tub filling slowly, Marie went back down to check on Lisa. Four pans were filled, and a large pot was nearly full.

"I need help with this one, Mom," Lisa said.

Marie removed the heavy pot and set it out of the way on the stove, then put one of the last empty pots under the spigot.

"Let's make sure to fill any water bottles, too." She reached up into the cupboard and removed several empty Nalgene water bottles they'd accumulated over the years. She carried them to the first floor bathroom and started to fill them one at a time.

With the tub faucet running upstairs and the sink faucet running in the kitchen, there was less pressure than normal in the downstairs bathroom, but the water still flowed[27].

Marie didn't know that their time was running out, but she was making the best of it. She had finished filling the water bottles and was out in the garage, looking for any large, empty containers she could use to store water, when she heard Lisa cry out.

"Mommy, the water stopped."

"Go ahead and turn the faucet off, and start finding the lids to those pots and pans. Make sure they're all covered up. And don't spill anything!" she called back.

Marie went over to the water heater and shined her flashlight on the pipes leading to and from the large tank. She followed one pipe to the left until she found a valve. She reached over and turned the lever the opposite direction. Then she followed another pipe and turned another valve. These valves effectively sealed off the water heater from the outside, turning it into a fifty-gallon water container. No water or anything else would be able to make it past these valves, and the water inside would be clean and safe to drink for a long time. And in the unlikely event that any sediment had shaken loose in the water heater, at the same time Jeff had purchased the "WaterBOB", he had also purchased a small device that fit on the drain valve on the bottom of the water tank. It was a simple water filter. If there was any contamination inside the tank, the water would still be clean after going through the filter.

Marie went back upstairs, unhooked the fill hose from the tub faucet, and sealed the bag. It was nearly full, and contained about 90 gallons. They definitely wouldn't die of thirst, but would they be able to survive whatever else was coming?

16. Cashing In

Luis walked around the neighborhood with a new attitude. He was the king of all he surveyed. Instead of trying to keep a low profile, he walked with brash confidence.

Just moments ago, a woman had come running out of her house, clutching her cell phone, shouting at him.

"Does your cell phone work? Mine doesn't! My regular phone doesn't either. I need to call my husband — he's working in Seattle today. I have to talk to him. Can you help me?" Her eyes were full of tears and she was shaking slightly.

Luis said "Sorry, I don't have a cell phone," and watched as she immediately ran to the nearest house and started pounding on the door. It was interesting and unusual. Someone had asked him for help. That hadn't ever happened before, and it gave him a feeling of power.

Luis kept walking, thinking about the important piece of information he had just gained. No phones worked. This meant there would be no annoying calls made to the police if anyone wasn't happy with him walking around the neighborhood.

Luis didn't know why the phones weren't working[28], but it didn't matter — his conclusion was still correct. Nobody was able to call anyone else, and it would be that way for a long time to come.

Two minutes later, Luis saw an elderly man step out of his house and quickly walk across the street to the broken front window of the house facing his. He heard him call "Are you OK, Edna?"

"Help!" he'd heard someone reply from inside. The old man walked quickly to the front door of the house, opened it, and went inside. Luis kept walking, with no desire to waste time on rescuing anyone. After all, he could spend the whole day trying to rescue people, and what would he get for it? Nothing.

Luis walked with a purpose from house to house, occasionally stopping in front of one, staring at the front windows, even walking up and looking in from time to time. He'd seen startled faces inside, looking back at the man who had suddenly appeared in their window, and he'd just waved and continued walking. For all they knew, he was trying to see if they needed help. There was no problem. There was nothing they could do about it.

He didn't bother with the houses that had partially or fully collapsed. He'd heard cries for help from more than one of them, and had seen the faces of some of the people huddled outside. Many of these houses would be deathtraps.

Three times so far, he'd also passed houses that were on fire. Natural gas lines had torn loose, and until all the pressure in the line dissipated, gas leaked out and filled up spaces in damaged homes. Unfortunately, some of those spaces also had a source of ignition: a pilot light that was still burning in a stove or water heater, a small fire that had resulted from electrical wires short-circuiting before the power went out, or maybe even someone lighting a cigarette, hoping to relax after all of the excitement. The result was the same, though — the natural gas ignited, initially creating an explosion and leaving a burning building behind. Luis actually heard an explosion at one point, several blocks away[29].

In the neighborhood Luis was currently scouting, the lots were often large, and most houses had a full front and back yard, with plenty of space between houses. And since there wasn't any breeze at the time, the fires had mostly been isolated to the houses where they had started. Only twice so far had Luis seen more than one house burning at a time, probably because they had been built too close together. The recent rain probably also made a big difference, keeping the asphalt shingle and cedar shake roofs from quickly bursting into flames when burning embers from a neighboring fire had drifted over and landed on them.

Even in the midst of this destruction, many houses were more or less intact. Either because they had been built more recently or gone through an earthquake retrofit, there were plenty of safe-looking buildings for Luis to loot.

To improve the situation even more, Luis noticed a change in architecture as he walked three more blocks south. The houses in this area were newer and in much better shape. In fact, aside from an occasional broken window, none of them appeared to be seriously damaged.

At this point, Luis had been able to stare at many houses and frightened people without having to worry about anyone's response. His confidence grew with each house he passed, and now it was built up enough to take action. It was time to get rich. Few people were outdoors, so everyone else was inside and relatively safe, or gone because they left earlier and hadn't been able to make their way back. Luis felt his heart beat faster as he anticipated his next move.

It only took a few minutes for him to find the perfect house. There was an Audi in the driveway, several broken windows, and no sign of anyone home. Maybe the family had left for the day in another vehicle. In this neighborhood, nearly everyone had two or more vehicles. He walked calmly up to the large, broken front window and called inside, as he'd seen the old man doing earlier.

"Is everyone OK in there?" There was no reply. He called again, more loudly. There was still no reply. Good — this meant nobody was home. He walked to the front door and tried it. It was locked. This was no problem. He walked around to the back of the house and grinned widely as he saw the shattered sliding glass door. This was a sign, he thought. It was calling out to him to come inside and have a look around.

Luis walked through the opening and called out again, "Is everyone OK? I'm here to help." There was still no response. It was time to go to work. Falling back on his burglary skills, Luis began to scan for valuables, ignoring the kitchen and moving to the living room.

That's where Luis saw him. A man's hips and legs stuck out from underneath a collapsed, heavy-looking bookshelf, and Luis could see a pool of blood on the hardwood floor. The man had to be dead. Luis got down on his hands and knees to peer under the edge of the shelf, but couldn't see anything. "Hey man, are you alive under there?" He poked the man's leg with one finger. The man didn't move and didn't make a sound.

It was time to move on. There was no use wasting time on a corpse, and if this guy wasn't dead, he was close to it. There was nothing Luis could do about it. That bookcase probably weighed a ton. Luis resumed his scan of the house. He made his way upstairs, looked through an office, quickly looked over what appeared to be a guest bedroom, and entered the master bedroom. He'd had good luck with master bedrooms before. Many people wanted to sleep near their valuables. He looked under the bed, in the nightstand drawers, in the dresser drawers — nothing besides some papers. Then he searched the closet. High on the top shelf, he found a shoebox.

This could be good. Most people didn't store their shoes in boxes on the top shelf, in his experience. He pulled it down, opened it up, and looked inside. There was a passport, a variety of documents, and a cloth bag with a zipper on it. He pulled out the cloth bag, dropping the shoebox to the floor. He unzipped the bag, and using the dim light that filtered through the bedroom window, he peered inside. It was stuffed with cash.

17. Cleaning Up

Marie turned the scanner off to conserve its battery. She'd been listening to local fire and police dispatch operators calling the officers and firefighters on their radio systems, telling them about various emergencies, injuries, fires, and other problems in the area[30].

She didn't need to hear any more. Based on the responses, and more importantly, the lack of response, it was clear to her that any remaining police or fire personnel were completely overwhelmed. In the short time she'd been listening, she'd heard calls for help from four different fires, and the response had been the same in every case. "We don't have the resources. Everyone else is either missing or dealing with other life-threatening issues."

Marie knew that they were on their own, and listening to the details any more would only depress her and probably scare Lisa, so now the scanner sat quietly.

The ham radio was still on though. Marie was hoping that Jeff and Robbie would call her on it. The laptop that she'd used earlier to show their coordinates on the Internet map was shut off too, to conserve its battery. There was no connection to the Internet anyway. If their local Internet service provider was still providing access, it didn't really matter because there was currently no power available to run the cable modem or the wireless router that distributed the signal throughout the house. For now, they were essentially cut off from the world[31], aside from their radios and face-to-face conversations they could have with people in the neighborhood.

Now was a good time to see how the neighbors were doing, Marie thought. She found Lisa, who was industriously sweeping up the last of the small pieces of the broken plate into a dustpan.

"Let's go check on the neighbors[32] and make sure they're OK."

Marie and Lisa walked outside, stood on the front porch, and looked around. If they looked to the right, blocking out the view of two collapsed carports down the street, it almost looked like a normal scene. Some things were wrong, though. Two of the neighbors' dogs were barking non-stop. That would get annoying after a while, Marie thought, hoping that someone would calm them down soon. The car alarms had stopped going off, and most of the sirens they'd heard in the distance had stopped, too. The dogs must be upset by something else. Maybe it was just fear and excitement in general, or maybe they could sense that the earth was still shifting under them, and they were trying to give warning. Marie didn't want to think about that.

"Let's go check on the Johnsons," Marie said, taking Lisa's hand. They started crossing the street, then paused in the middle to take another look up and down. Several hundred yards away, Marie could see a column of smoke rising, and the faint sounds of shouting carried through the still air. She hoped the people there weren't in danger, but there was nothing she could do for someone that far away, not yet anyway. She needed to make sure her immediate neighbors were safe.

They finished crossing the street and walked up to the Johnsons' front door. Marie knocked and seconds later, Larry Johnson, a retired mechanic and one of the more friendly neighbors in their area, opened the door with a concerned look on his face.

"Are you all OK?" he asked quickly.

"Yes, are you and Bonnie?" Marie asked back.

"Yeah, but she's pretty shaken up." His eyebrows wrinkled for a second. "No pun intended," he added with a wry smile. "We have a lot of fallen shelves, broken dishes. And our new TV is smashed, but it looks like we wouldn't be able to use it anyway. We don't have any power. But it made an awful mess. Broken glass is everywhere."

"Did your gas leak? Did you need to shut it off? Did you get some water stored before it stopped?"

"Yes, yes and yes," Larry replied. "I didn't think the water would last long, so I filled up some big containers." He paused for another second before asking: "Where are Jeff & Robbie?"

"They're up in the mountains," Marie answered. "I hope they're OK, but I have no idea. I'm hoping they'll call in soon on the radio. Oops, that reminds me, I should get the handheld radio and keep it with me, so I don't miss their call. We should get going. Are you going to check on Mrs. Mackey next door?"

"Yeah, in just a couple minutes we'll have things wrapped up here, and I'll start checking on other neighbors."

"OK, see you later." Marie took Lisa and returned to the house for the handheld radio.

18. Climbing

Robbie walked into the clearing, where his father was waiting, just over the edge of the cliff on the other side. Even though the route from the truck was uphill, Robbie covered the distance faster this time than the first time, earlier in the day. He kept telling himself "Dad needs you — don't let him down! No whining. Push it all the way up the hill!" And he did. The lighter pack helped, but his injured, trapped father really depending on him. That gave him all the energy he needed.

"Dad! I'm back!" he called, as he walked toward the cliff and tried to catch his breath.

"Great. Nothing new down here," Jeff called from the ledge. "I'm ready to come up now! Can you see anywhere to tie the rope?"

"I'm looking around now."

Robbie looked around and saw a large rock nearby. He could tell that it had fallen from the mountain above, during the earthquake because the ground around it was freshly disturbed. But would it hold his father's weight? He walked up to it, pushed on it from different sides, and it didn't budge. It looked like it would work. And either way, this would have to work. There was no other place to attach the rope.

"I've got a big rock up here that I can tie to, Dad. That looks like the only good option."

"OK, do it."

Robbie tied off the rope, using a figure eight knot, which his father taught him to tie last summer when they went rock climbing. He usually wasn't that good with knots, but this one stuck in his head because he had used it several times since then. Maybe it wasn't the perfect knot for this job, but he was certain it wouldn't slip, and right now that was most important. Robbie remembered one rock climber they had met who described the knot as "bomb-proof." That may have been a slight exaggeration, but it was a good description. "Earthquake-proof" would be good enough for now, Robbie thought to himself. Either way, it would work[33].

Robbie made the figure eight in the rope, walked the free end around the base of the large rock, and then fed that free end back through the figure eight. He tightened it up and made sure it looked right. It was a solid knot. Then he added two half-hitches with the remaining two feet of rope that he already fed through, just as if he was tying the rope into a climbing harness. This was a knot he would bet his life on. Double-bomb-proof, he told himself.

"Dad, I tied a figure eight on the rock up here, and I'm going to lower the rope." Robbie grabbed the rest of the coil of rope and scooted up to the edge of the cliff. He looked over and saw his father looking up.

"I'm ready — hand it down." Robbie dropped the rope over the edge into his father's open hands. "Oh wait — let's get this stuff up there now." Jeff packaged up the sleeping bag and mat. Robbie dropped down the end of the cord he'd used earlier, and a minute later he hauled the gear back up over the edge and placed it to one side.

"Now throw me the end of the cord again," Jeff said. "I need to tie a different knot."

Robbie dropped the cord down again. "What are you going to do with it?"

"Remember the Prusik knot?" Jeff asked? He quickly measured a piece of cord, cut it, and tied the short piece to the rope, fashioning a loop that angled out sideways, away from the rope. This was a unique knot. The loop would tighten and grip the rope firmly when weight was placed in it, but when the weight was removed, the loop would loosen its grip and could slide farther up or down the rope. This knot would allow Jeff to stand on the rope with one foot, sliding that foot up as he progressed. It was an effective, movable foot-hold.

Robbie remembered tying the knot a couple times last summer, but knew he wouldn't have been able to tie it now without some help. He was glad his dad remembered. He'd have to practice that knot again when they got home. *If* they got home, he thought grimly.

"OK, I'm going to tie the end of the rope to this small rock, to help keep the rest of the rope from coming along as I pull the Prusik knot up. We'll still be able to pull the rope up later." Jeff tied the rope to a small, foot-long chunk of rock resting on the ledge nearby. Then he said "OK, here I come. Give me some space when I get to the top."

Jeff put his foot in the Prusik loop, then stood up on the loop, pulling himself up with his arms at the same time. He let his right foot hang behind him; he didn't want to injure it further. He stood with his weight on his left foot in the loop, and reached higher with his hands. He held on tightly, shook his left foot gently until the loop loosened its hold on the rope, and slowly pulled the loop upward along the rope by lifting his left foot. The rock tied to the end of the rope served its purpose, keeping some tension on the rope, which allowed Jeff to pull the loop up without pulling the rest of the rope up, too.

Having moved up about two feet, Jeff was once again able to put his weight on his left foot, as the loop gripped the rope. Jeff repeated these movements until he was up to the edge of the cliff.

"Just a little farther Dad!"

Jeff pulled himself up to the lip of the cliff, then pulled himself over. He winced in pain as he pulled his right leg over and bumped his foot on a protruding rock. Then he lay on the ground, panting.

"Welcome back, Dad," Robbie said. Seeing his father in front of him was an incredible relief.

Jeff sat up, still breathing hard, and smiled. "I'm glad to be back."

Very carefully, Jeff stood up, gingerly balancing on his left foot. Robbie couldn't resist. He stepped forward and hugged him, squeezing hard. He could feel tears in his eyes, and he did his best to hold them back.

"I was worried, Dad."

"I was too, son."

"I'm still worried about Mom and Lisa."

"I am too. Let's figure out how I'm going to walk, and then let's get out of here. We're going to have a busy afternoon."

"Maybe you should sit and rest for a minute."

Jeff looked surprised. "You're right. I should." He paused for a moment. "I'm not used to you giving me orders," he said, grinning.

"Well, maybe I'm in charge now," Robbie said, grinning back.

Robbie quickly pulled up the rest of the rope and untied the rock. He untied the loop his father had used as a foothold, put it to the side, and started coiling up the rope.

"We need to find a crutch," Jeff said. "Otherwise, I don't think I'll be able to walk down. And I know I can't hop all the way down."

"Let me look," Robbie said. He finished coiling up the rope and set it next to his pack. Then he scoured the area until he found a six-foot-long branch that had a smaller branch forking off near one end. He dragged it back to Jeff. "How about this?"

"That'll work," Jeff said. Jeff stood up and balanced as he measured the level of his armpit and compared it to the height of the fork in the stick. It was about two feet too long. He took his Leatherman[34] tool out of its belt sheath and opened the small, sharp saw blade. In less than a minute, he had sawed through the end of the stick at an angle, so it would have a sharp end and would be less likely to slip going down the trail. Then he sawed off most of the protruding side branch, creating a "Y" at the top.

"Grab me that piece of 550 cord I used earlier," Jeff said. Robbie retrieved it. Jeff used the knife blade on his Leatherman tool to cut the cord into two sections. Then he took Robbie's fleece jacket, rolled it up, and tied it into the top of the "Y" with the two lengths of cord. He slowly stood up and rested his weight on the improvised pad, testing his new crutch.

"This will work. Let's go," Jeff said.

Robbie finished packing the remaining gear into his backpack. "OK Dad, ready."

They started down the trail.

Five minutes later, as they slowly worked their way down the mountain, both of them were surprised as their radios simultaneously squawked.

"This is the emergency broadcast system. This is not a test. Washington's Governor, Arthur Masterson, has declared a state of emergency, and has requested immediate assistance from the National Guard as well as FEMA, the Federal Emergency Management Administration, to help with emergency rescue operations in the region. Widespread power outages and roadways blocked by gridlocked traffic or debris have hampered rescue efforts. Residents are advised to turn off their natural gas at the meter, and to stay in their homes, as long as their homes are undamaged and no gas is leaking. Red Cross rescue shelters are being set up. There are scattered reports of looting in some areas of Seattle. If you see any

looters, leave the area immediately. More information will follow shortly."

They continued walking. "Wow. They're looting already," Jeff said. "That was pretty quick. You should turn off your radio to save the battery. We only need one turned on at a time now."

Robbie turned off his radio and stopped for a moment to put it back in his pack. He didn't say anything. He was getting tired, but even more than being tired, he was worried about his mother and sister. He wondered if there were any looters in his neighborhood, and if the house was even still standing.

Jeff looked at Robbie as they continued walking. He could tell that Robbie was worried. "Don't worry, Robbie. Mom and Lisa can take care of themselves. Your mother is tough and smart, and our house is sturdy. They'll be OK."

Robbie worried anyway. As they continued to walk, Robbie took a moment to pray silently, "God, please take care of my mother and sister." He didn't know what else to say, and left it at that. He could feel tears welling up in his eyes again, and this time he just let them leak out as he walked. It didn't last too long, and he felt a little bit better. He wiped his face and looked to the side. His father's eyes appeared to be damp. Jeff glanced over at Robbie, and it was clear that he had tears in his eyes too. Neither of them said a word. There was no need to. They continued walking.

A couple minutes later, Jeff handed his radio to Robbie. "I can't use this thing and use my crutch at the same time. Can you scan the AM and FM stations to see what else we can hear?"

Robbie switched the radio to the AM band, and started scanning. Occasional static came out of the small speaker, but nothing else. He switched to FM and continued scanning. Eventually the radio locked onto a radio station out of Eastern Washington.

"There are reports of a major earthquake in the Seattle area, at least 7.6 on the Richter scale. The governor has declared a state of emergency. Many of the roadways into and out of the city are blocked, the power is out for millions of residents, and emergency services are overwhelmed..."

Jeff and Robbie listened as they walked. There was no new news, only what they'd heard already. It was really bad, and they needed to get back home as soon as possible. Robbie tried finding another station, but reception was poor. The most powerful radio stations in the area probably didn't function any more due to the earthquake. Eventually, Robbie stopped trying to find any other stations and left the radio on the frequency they'd heard earlier.

The trip back to the truck was slow because Jeff needed to use the crutch carefully. He eventually got into a good rhythm, and about an hour and a half later, they reached the end of the trail. They came out into the open area and saw the parking lot. Their truck sat there, untouched since Robbie had been there only a little while ago. Jeff opened the doors and Robbie loaded up their bags and the rope. They started to get into the truck to leave, when Jeff stopped and looked at Robbie with a thoughtful expression on his face.

"Robbie, we have a small problem. I should have thought of this earlier. I don't think I'll be able to drive..."

19. Driving

Jeff looked down at his right foot. "If I try to drive using my right foot, I'll destroy my ankle. And even in a splint, I don't think I'll be able to put enough pressure on it to push the gas pedal down enough to get us going. Let's see what happens when I use my left foot."

Jeff sat in the driver's seat, gingerly lifted his right foot up and around the floor pedals, and then attempted to press the gas and brake pedals with his left foot. He gasped in pain. Pressing the brake wasn't a problem, but when he tried to push down on the gas pedal, he couldn't do it without putting pressure on his injured ankle, which was wedged up and to the right. Because of the raised floor between the driver and passenger areas, there was no place to safely put his right foot without causing more pain.

"This is definitely a problem," Jeff said.

"Then what will we do?" Robbie asked.

Jeff looked at him. "Guess."

Robbie stared at him for a moment. "I'm driving, right?"

"Yep."

Robbie felt a sinking feeling in his stomach. "Uh... But I don't know how to drive."

"You're smart and you learn fast, so I'll teach you."

Robbie beamed at the compliment, but didn't stop his questioning, and didn't make him any less worried.

"How will you teach me when you can't even show me?"

"I'll talk you through it," Jeff said.

Robbie looked at him with wide eyes. "So you're going to talk me through an entire driver's education course in the next few minutes?" Robbie had been looking forward to taking a Driver's Education class, getting his learner's permit, and all the other stuff that came with getting ready to drive around like adults did. He never expected to learn like this.

"Yep." Jeff nodded slowly.

"We don't have a choice, I think," Robbie said. "We might as well get started."

"Like I said, you learn fast. This is our only way out. Get in the driver's seat and let's get started."

Robbie sat in the driver's seat and started by adjusting the seat so that he was comfortable and could reach the pedals. "Adjust your mirrors so you can see," Jeff said. "You need to see what's happening behind you and on both sides." Robbie adjusted the side mirrors, then the rearview mirror. Now he had a clear view behind the truck without having to crane his neck.

Jeff quickly explained what the gas pedal and brakes did.

"Come on, Dad. I've been playing Gran Turismo forever. I know how those work."

"Sorry — just trying to be thorough," Jeff said with a smile. "Since the truck has an automatic transmission, you don't have to worry about shifting gears until we're on the highway, or if we want to go in reverse. That makes it easy."

"Like I said," Robbie repeated with exasperation, "I played the video game. Same thing."

Jeff took the interruption in stride and continued his quick lesson, still attempting to be thorough, talking Robbie through braking, turning and operating the gears.

"Now put the transmission in '3'. That's third gear," Jeff said.

"Drive over to the other side of the parking lot. On the way, brake gently, then accelerate again, then brake again when we get close to the edge of the lot. I know it sounds a little silly, but it'll give you an idea of how the truck feels when you brake and accelerate."

Robbie followed the instructions with no difficulties. Maybe video games were good for more than just developing hand-eye coordination, he thought. But this definitely wasn't the time to convince his dad to spend more time in front of the TV playing games, if they still even had a functioning TV. He kept the thought to himself.

Jeff showed Robbie how to drive in reverse, back to where they had started. That was enough for now.

Jeff smiled. "Ready to get moving?"

"Are you serious? Is that the course?" Robbie asked. "If I knew it was this easy, I would have been bugging you start driving a long time ago."

"It's definitely not this easy. We have a long way to go before you're a safe driver, but we have to get home as soon as we can. This means some of your training will be 'on the job'. You'll learn as we go. Now aim the truck down the road, and we'll very slowly take some turns so you can get the feel for that."

As Robbie slowly accelerated, Jeff said "Did I ever tell you about my first experience driving? I didn't have a good feel for how the car steered, and I drove it right into a ditch as soon as I needed to make my first sharp turn. No joke. My first turn ever, and I dumped it right into a ditch. I sure felt stupid. And here's the worse part," Jeff continued as Robbie drove carefully down the bumpy road. "My buddy, whose car I had just put in the ditch, called his brother to get a truck to tow it out. We wanted to hurry, before the sheriff came by to give him a ticket. He hooked a chain to the car and started pulling it out, and slid the back of the truck into the same ditch. We had to get another truck to pull them both out. And I got to stand there the whole time, feeling like an idiot. We laughed pretty hard once we finally got out of the ditch. And we were lucky — the sheriff never did come by." He paused for moment. "Let's make sure you don't do that. I'm sure you can easily do better than I did."

"Yeah, Dad. I think it'll be easy to do better than that," Robbie said with a laugh. Jeff's story lightened the mood for the moment.

Robbie did quite a bit better than Jeff on his first attempt at driving. He didn't drive into any ditches or hit any trees on the way out. When they reached the paved road, Robbie moved the transmission lever to "D" for highway driving. They were finally on their way home.

20. Ready to Pounce

Luis kept walking, energized by his latest score. But the excitement didn't keep him from noticing that he was getting hungry and thirsty again.

He had just passed a house where the chimney had collapsed, and a man was shoveling debris off his driveway. This neighborhood wasn't in terrible shape. Nobody was screaming, and nothing was on fire. No houses in this area had collapsed, but some were seriously damaged. Nonetheless, nobody asked him for help as he walked by. These people had no idea that he had just broken into a house in their neighborhood, but they did notice something. Maybe it was the way he walked, or what he was wearing, or his style of haircut — something was different. He didn't know what it was, and didn't really care, but he recognized their looks. He'd seen them before, when walking around in some of the better neighborhoods near one of his foster homes in Chicago. He didn't fit into some places, and this was one of them.

The area he had walked through about ten minutes ago didn't look nearly this good. Just a few blocks to the north, he had seen many more broken windows, and several houses had partially or completely collapsed. He saw one house that probably would have survived the quake, except that a large tree had fallen and crushed the front left corner and a car that had been sitting in the driveway. And from one of the houses, he had even heard someone calling for help, but he pretended not to hear and kept walking. Someone else would help soon enough, and he didn't have time.

He passed another fine-looking house, and he could see past the side into the back yard. He stopped and looked at a woman standing near a gas grill. Then the smell hit him. They were barbecuing. The delicious aroma of sizzling beef made him salivate. What the heck were they doing, barbecuing now? He thought for a second, and guessed that they didn't want their food to spoil, and had just decided to cook it up now. And he wanted some.

He took a step toward the house, and stopped when the front door opened. A man walked through the doorway, carrying a bag of trash. The man paused when he saw Luis and turned slightly to face him, looking at him with a clear, direct gaze that wasn't hostile or friendly. This man was clearly not afraid of Luis, and while he may be generous enough to give some food to a stranger, Luis didn't want to endure any questions about what he was doing here, where he was going, or why his pockets appeared to be so full. Luis turned and kept walking. The man watched him as he continued down the block.

While the food smelled great, more than anything, Luis was thirsty. All of this walking had worn him out. He had already walked more today than in the last couple months put together, and the beer he drank earlier didn't rehydrate him at all. As he daydreamed for a moment, he thought about catching a bus to the nearest mall, where he could start to spend some of his money, get something good to drink, maybe buy a new pair of shoes... but then he remembered how bad things were. The mall was probably shut down. And the buses were probably stuck. In fact, when Luis had crossed one street just a few minutes ago and looked toward the main street, he saw that it appeared to be completely jammed, with many cars stopped in both directions. All of the drivers were probably getting thirsty too, he thought, as he swallowed dryly.

Luis kept walking down that block, and then another, looking for a house that was clearly unoccupied. There had to be a few decent houses around here where nobody was home, he thought, and with no neighbors like that guy he had seen a few minutes ago.

Five minutes later, he passed a two-story, tan house, and it looked like a good candidate. Although the front was clear of any bushes that could hide a break-in, there was a fence and gate, and the fence appeared to extend to the back yard, as far as he could see. If he could get into the back yard, he could probably break in comfortably, out of view of the neighbors. He continued walking, just to play it safe.

Two minutes later, Luis changed direction and walked back the way he had come, taking another look and trying not to attract attention. On this second pass, he saw a woman come out of the house and a girl standing in the doorway, looking out at the street with wide eyes. The woman was carrying a garbage bag that sounded like it contained broken glass when she unceremoniously dumped it onto the front porch, off to the side.

Luis started to apply his limited mental resources to assess the situation. This was the nicest house on the block. There was a car in the driveway. He could use that to get away with whatever he took. There was a woman hauling broken glass outside, and a girl in the doorway. Luis figured that if she was doing the cleanup, there was probably no man around for now.

Luis didn't process every piece of information consciously. Instead he made the decision with his gut. This was the house. This was his next target. Maybe he could eventually find another house in the area that was empty, but he had a good feeling about this one. It was time to spice things up a bit. What did he have to worry about anyhow? The odds of actually getting caught now were almost zero. It was time to go big or go home. He could get something to drink, maybe a nice dinner, take a load off of his tired feet, and maybe much more.

21. Coming Home

"Dad, do you think Mom and Lisa are OK?"

"I'm sure they are, and we'll see them soon."

"Can we call them on the cell phone?"

"Let me check the signal and see."

Jeff took his phone from the backpack and turned it on. He waited. No signal. "I think we had a signal when we were here previously. So this means that either the cell tower that covers this area has no power or the equipment is damaged. We can try again later. Maybe another tower is working. Let's try the radio."

Jeff listened and tried transmitting as Robbie drove. He heard nothing. The repeater they'd been able to access earlier in the day was apparently not working.[35]

"Let's scan the other frequencies I have programmed in here." Jeff pressed a button, and the radio started switching from one frequency to the next. If it detected a transmission in progress on a frequency, it would stop and allow Jeff to listen further.

The radio stopped several times on frequencies that had people talking on them, but Robbie and Jeff couldn't make out what was being said; there was too much static.

They continued driving down out of the mountains. When they were about a mile from the highway, the radio stopped on a station they could hear.

"—lots of houses on fire in that area and I heard there was some kind of landslide."

"Are you OK?"

"Yeah, I'm OK, but I don't know what to do. It looks so bad down there."

"I have to go. My wife needs me. Talk to you later. Stay safe."

Jeff pressed the transmit button, eager to jump in and talk to one of them before they left their radios.

At the same moment, as they rounded a bend in the road, Robbie slammed on the brakes. His short training session hadn't prepared him for anything like this, but he was able to act on instinct. The truck's anti-lock brakes kicked in and the truck stuttered forward as the wheels lost and regained traction several times per second. Robbie sat behind the wheel with his right foot locked forward on the brake, arms rigid and eyes wide, with the steering wheel locked in place. He could do nothing but wait. Wait. Wait... *Crash*! They hit the side of a fallen tree that lay across the roadway, blocking it completely.

Jeff had been focused on the radio and hadn't been paying attention to the road. The impact almost smashed his head against the dashboard. His seatbelt locked into place as soon as the forward momentum suddenly slowed, and it kept him from getting a bloody nose or worse. Robbie's seatbelt also worked as expected and he wasn't injured either. They both heard the tinkling sound of falling, broken glass, and they turned at the same time and looked at each other.

"I'm glad I was going slowly around that corner," Robbie said with a trembling voice, noticing that his hands and forehead were sweaty all of the sudden. He slowly pried his damp right hand off the steering wheel. It almost felt like it had been glued on because he was gripping it so tightly. He put the transmission in park. The engine was still running. Then he pried off his left hand and took a deep breath. "Wow. That was close."

Jeff took some deep breaths and relaxed his grip on the arm rest. "Yeah... wow." He paused and took another breath, trying to calm himself. "Thanks for driving slowly. You probably saved us both from a much worse accident. And since you were able to brake for a few yards, we didn't hit hard enough to make the airbags go off, which would have probably been a real drag. Let's take a look at the damage."

Jeff carefully got out of the truck, and using his crutch, hobbled to the front of the truck. Robbie came around the other side and looked at the front. The bumper was pushed slightly downward, and a protruding branch had cracked the headlight and crushed the turn signal on the passenger side.

"Go pop the hood," Jeff instructed. "It's the lever on the far left side, down low. Robbie pulled the latch, and Jeff pushed up the hood and looked inside.

"I don't see any branches sticking in here. Any on your side?"

"Nothing," Robbie said.

"This is good," Jeff said, "as much as crashing into a tree could be good. This could have been far worse. Let me check under the front real quick and see if anything else might be damaged." Jeff slowly lowered himself to the ground and looked under the front of the truck. Aside from the ends of some branches on the ground, it appeared to be clear of debris. He stood up and looked around a little more.

"This is odd," Jeff said. "Look at this." He pointed to the tree. "And this." He pointed to the ground nearby. There were long, fresh-looking gouges in the side of the tree, and broken glass on the ground, but about two feet away from where their truck had hit the tree. The glass wasn't from their truck.

"What's that from?" Robbie asked. "Oh wait — I bet I know."

"What?" Jeff asked.

"Someone else hit the tree." He thought for a second longer. "One of the other cars from the parking lot. Or both of them. They hit the tree, too."

"I think you're right," Jeff said. "But they obviously didn't keep going through here, so where did they go?"

"Let's look at the map," Robbie said. They unfolded their map on the truck's hood and looked at it.

"There," Jeff pointed at the map. "They must have backtracked to take this side road, and…." He traced his finger along the road, looking for where it would intersect with the paved road again.

"Wow," Robbie said. "That's a long way around."

Jeff consulted the legend and made a quick estimate. "Yeah, they probably had to go about fifty miles out of their way, assuming they want to go back to I-90 like we do. And that's a rough road, so they'll have to go slowly. At least two hours, probably three. And that's if the road isn't blocked up there, too. If there's a landslide or another tree, then they're in big trouble, especially if their gas tanks aren't full."

Three more hours? Robbie's heart fell. Would they ever get home?

22. The Tree

"How are we going to move this tree?" Robbie asked. "The truck barely moved it at all, so pushing on it will be pointless. And driving into it again could mess up the truck, and then we'll really be in trouble."

"What else can we do?" Jeff asked, watching Robbie's response. He loved watching Robbie learn to think for himself, and even when they were in a hurry, he gave Robbie at least a quick opportunity to learn something. It was a habit, and it usually only took a second or two longer than explaining it himself. And more and more often, Robbie would think of something that Jeff hadn't.

Robbie thought for a moment. "Well, we need to get the tree out of the way. We could use the saw on your multi-tool, but that would take forever. Do you have anything else we can cut the tree with? Hey — don't you have a hatchet or something in the back of the truck? I remember from the last time we went car-camping with Mom and Sis."

"Just what I was thinking," said Jeff with a grin. "Great minds think alike. Look under the back seat on the driver side. There should be a small axe under there."

Robbie found the axe. Its handle was a little over three feet long, and the head had a leather cover on it. He unsnapped it as he returned to the front of the truck, where Jeff waited.

Jeff took the axe. "Stand back. I'm going to get this started for you, but you'll need to work on it. It's tough to swing an axe with a messed up ankle." He gave the tree several whacks, and on the last swing, a large chunk of wood flew out. He handed the axe to Robbie and said "Your turn. Do it like I just did."

Robbie hacked at the tree for several minutes. It was harder work than he thought it would be, even with a sharp axe. Soon, he began to sweat, and the axe got heavier. At first he felt like he was just making a series of cuts in the log that wouldn't accomplish anything. But eventually, he started to figure out how to intersect the cuts, to cause larger and larger pieces of wood to fall free. Each time he swung, more chips of wood flew out. At last, as he got closer to cutting all the way through, he heard the tree creak.

"Good job. But stop now and stand back," said Jeff. "There's a lot of pressure built up with the branches that are all pressed down by the weight of the trunk. They could cause part of the tree to spring up[36] and hurt you. Let me help finish that for you."

Jeff took the axe and Robbie backed up toward the middle of the truck. Jeff looked at the tree for a minute, examining how the branches were compressed, poking some of them with the end of the axe. He chopped sideways along the length of the log, until he had cut through several of the branches that had been pinned to the ground. With the last cut, the end of the branch closest to the trunk snapped downward, away from Jeff, with a large "*Thwack*!" The tree slowly creaked some more.

"OK, we're almost done. A couple more chops." Jeff hacked down into the cut on the log once, twice, and the trunk split in two. The upper section of the tree sprung upward about a foot, and the lower section stayed where it was, since most of the tension had been relieved by chopping off some of the pinned branches. "We're almost ready to get going. See if you can push the top of the tree out of the way."

Robbie walked to the other side of the tree and pulled on a branch on the top section that had recently been chopped free. The top of the tree moved! And then it stopped. He pulled harder. It wouldn't budge.

"Wait a second," Jeff said. "There's one branch that's jammed." He hopped over to one of the branches and took a look. He handed the axe to Robbie. "Go for it."

With Robbie's new lumberjacking skills, he made short work of the branch, severing it in three short chops.

"Try now," Jeff said.

Grunting and pushing with all of his strength, Robbie was able to move the heavy section out of the way. He pushed it all the way over to the side of the road and made sure there was enough room for the truck to get by.

"Let's go," said Jeff.

Robbie slowly backed the truck up about ten yards, then changed gears and drove forward, carefully guiding the truck around the rest of the trunk poking into the roadway. They were back on track.

After about 15 minutes, they reached Interstate-90. Robbie stepped on the brakes as the highway came into view. It was a nightmare.

23. Disaster Area

With the Cascade Mountains to the east, Lake Washington sitting between Seattle and Bellevue, and the waterways of the Puget Sound to the west, there were very few major routes out of Seattle. I-90 was the only way to go east for many people. With this as the obvious option, it only took about two hours for it to become completely filled with fleeing vehicles. In addition to locals trying to get out, knowing that their destroyed homes weren't worth sticking around for, there was the added problem of the several thousand people who were only in town for the baseball game. Hotels previously jammed to capacity were transformed into dangerous, dark, stinking caves, some with serious structural damage and all without power to run the air conditioning or running water to flush the toilets.

To make matters worse, gas pumps no longer functioned, even if people somehow found a way to pay. More and more cars were running out of gas as they sat in traffic, engines running, waiting, hoping for the road ahead of them to magically clear up.

Occasionally, a few people would work together to push a vehicle to the shoulder so that others could crawl past, but for the most part, drivers kept pressing forward. It didn't take long before the cars with empty tanks were effectively pinned in, solidifying the gridlock. It was getting worse and worse. The clogged roadway started in Seattle and continued through

Bellevue to the east, toward Snoqualmie pass, the last real bottleneck on the way to Eastern Washington.

Robbie and Jeff sat in the truck on the shoulder of the onramp overlooking the highway, and stared in amazement at the honking flood of vehicles inching eastward. They even saw a two RV's with Mariners flags hanging limply.

"Dad, what's going on? " Jeff cracked the passenger window, and they could hear the honking clearly now.

"Well, they probably realize things won't be back to normal in the city for a while, and their power and water and cell phones and TV's probably aren't working, so the only thing they can think to do is to get out of Dodge."

"Dodge? Huh?"

"It's an expression. I mean they'll want to get out[37] of the area, out of Seattle and Bellevue and the other towns around here. 'Get out of Dodge' is a saying from the old West."

"We're still going home, right?"

"Darn right, we are. We have to get back to our family. Your mom and sister are waiting for us. And we need to be together. A family belongs together."

It looked as if only a few people had the same idea, since there were only occasional cars visible driving westward, toward the disaster area[38].

"Let's go," Jeff said. Robbie pulled onto the highway, glad that they weren't trying to go the other way, but afraid of what lay ahead.

As Jeff scanned the airwaves for any more news or conversations that could reveal useful information about whatever was ahead of them, Robbie was thinking.

"Dad, why don't people leave town using both sides of the highway?"

Jeff stopped turning the dial and thought for a second. "You would think some people would be desperate enough to try, wouldn't you? Well, take a look at the area between both sides of the highway — the median. See how every so often you can see a car stuck in there? They probably tried getting across and got stuck. It's actually not that easy around here to just cut across the highway. But as traffic gets worse and worse, I bet more people will figure out how to cross without getting stuck. They may even spot one of those areas where the State Patrol can make U-turns. People will cross at those spots for sure. Eventually, it'll be just as hard to get into the city, because there will probably be a traffic jam on both sides of the road, both headed east. I-5, which goes north and south along this side of the state, is probably broken and impassable in many places.

Tacoma to the south and Everett to the north are probably in the same bad situation that Seattle is in. I-90 is probably one of the best ways out of the area. If Snoqualmie Pass isn't blocked by landslides, that is. Either way, we need to get home while our side of the highway is still usable. We'll be driving head-on into this mess. We need to keep going while we still can."

Robbie pushed down on the accelerator a bit harder as they turned toward Bellevue and whatever was waiting for them.

24. New Home

As soon as the door shut behind the woman, Luis walked quickly to the side gate, reached over for where he thought the latch would be, found it, released it, and opened the gate. He walked into the back yard and shut the gate behind him.

He quickly scanned and verified that his earlier assumption was correct. The fence extended around the entire back yard, so he was still covered from any neighbor's view. He walked up to the closest window and peered inside. It was blocked by a curtain, and since this was the side of the garage, he didn't expect to see anything interesting inside. At the same time, this could be the perfect place to break in, because the woman and girl were probably not in the garage. They were probably in the warmer living area, cleaning up the rest of the mess from the quake.

Before actually trying to break in, Luis decided to scout further, and he quietly walked around toward the back of the house and slowly poked his head around the corner. He could see a set of French doors that unfortunately weren't broken — being able to walk right in would have made things much easier. But he could see through them, and he slowly approached, to get a better view of what was happening inside the house, and to see what might be worth stealing.

As he peered through the side of the door, he saw a glimpse of the woman carrying a jug of water toward what must be the kitchen. The water reminded him of his dry mouth and powerful thirst. He looked down, along the base of the house, and saw what he had hoped was there, a water spigot. Why not get a drink and recharge before breaking in? He got down on all fours and slowly turned the spigot, waiting for some cool, fresh water to flow. He could already taste it. A few drops trickled out, and then... nothing. He turned the spigot farther. Nothing happened. There was no more water outside. Seeing the water inside made Luis even more determined to get in. If water was shut off everywhere, this may be the only place with stored water.

Luis waited and watched for another minute as the woman walking around busily, occasionally trailed by the girl. He was even more confident now that they were alone. Soon he would be the king of this castle. In a few minutes, he would be a much happier man.

He backtracked to the garage window he had seen first, grabbing a fist-sized rock from the flowerbed. He took off his hoodie and wrapped it around the rock, hoping to muffle the sound of breaking glass, and smashed it against the window.

As shards of glass fell to the floor inside the garage and shattered into smaller pieces, the sounds echoed through the garage and into the house, and Lisa heard them.

"Mom — it's happening again!" Lisa shrieked in terror.

Marie and Lisa instinctively braced themselves for a moment, then Marie grabbed Lisa's hand and started to move toward the front door, to get out of the house. Then she stopped. Nothing was moving. Nothing rumbled.

"What did you hear?" Marie asked.

"Glass breaking in the garage," Lisa replied.

"Maybe some things that shifted earlier finally fell," Marie said. "Since nothing is moving, it's not another earthquake, so I think we're OK for now. Come here."

Lisa stepped toward Marie and embraced her.

"It'll be OK baby," Marie said gently. "We'll be all right." She could feel Lisa relax slightly.

"Now I'll go check in the garage. Something probably fell down — nothing to worry about. But wait here just in case."

"OK, Mommy."

Marie walked down the hall and opened the door that led from the hallway to the garage.

25. Another Detour

Robbie and Jeff drove west on I-90 for about 25 minutes. While traffic in the opposite direction was heavy and often stopped, traffic back toward Seattle was almost nonexistent. They were both quiet, thinking about the crazy day they'd had, as well as wondering whether the women at home were safe, injured, busy, frightened, in need of help, or out helping others. Maybe they were downtown when the earthquake struck. Nobody wanted to think about that possibility.

As they drove past the city of North Bend, they were able to see about two hundred yards ahead before the highway curved to the right. Robbie pushed down with a bit more pressure on the accelerator, since the coast was clear.

Jeff continued to change the dial on the truck's radio, listening for any useful news. At the same time, he let the handheld ham radio scan a variety of frequencies, listening for news, eyewitness descriptions of what was going on, anything. The lack of information was beginning to wear on them both, and Jeff wanted to replace the worst-case scenarios playing out in his head with some real scenarios that weren't that bad.

Although radio stations around the state and country were all broadcasting information about the earthquake, none of them were getting up-to-the-minute updates, because nobody in the disaster area was able to communicate effectively yet. The government was still in complete disarray. Their reports were far too vague to help Jeff and Robbie understand what they were driving into. Either way, Jeff continued to scan, hoping to hear something useful.

As Robbie continued down the roadway, something ahead of them moved. It wasn't like the earlier confusion in the day, when the quake knocked him down. But with the extra adrenaline in his system, his awareness was heightened, and he lifted his foot from the accelerator. About 200 yards ahead of them, Robbie saw movement as the hillside started to move. A falling tree had alerted him like a waving flag.

Jeff sensed the change in velocity and looked up from the radio dial. His eyes widened and he cried out "Stop!"

However, even as Jeff was just starting to look upward, Robbie had already moved his foot to the brake pedal and started his downward stomp. Moments later, they had stopped completely, about thirty yards from the edge of the new wall of rocks, soil and trees that completely blocked this side of the highway.

"Dang it!" Jeff shouted. Once again their environment had transformed in front of their eyes.

Robbie sat there, head spinning, realizing that if he had been going just a bit faster, they could have been directly under the slide, they could have been trapped or hurt or… He didn't even want to think about it. He sat there with both hands on the wheel, heart pounding, not saying a word. In the back of his brain, he wondered how many surprises he could get in one day without having a heart attack. Sure, he was young and healthy, but this was ridiculous.

All three westbound lanes were covered with several feet of soil, boulders, and from what they could see, at least two large trees. Fortunately for the drivers moving away from the disaster zone, the blockage didn't extend past the median, so their path was still clear.

Instead of slowing down and rubbernecking, as most people do when they witness some kind of accident on the roadway, the drivers in the other lane continued driving as fast as they could. However, due to the heavy traffic, nobody was able to actually increase speed, so all that really changed was a significant increase in honking from cars that were approaching the landslide area. Many of the drivers worried that another landslide might block their side of the road too, so they honked in a futile effort to get the cars in front of them to hurry up and get out of their way. Traffic continued at a crawl.

Robbie and Jeff sat dumbfounded, staring at the thousands of tons of wall that had been placed directly in their path. Though Robbie's experience driving a four-wheel-drive truck could be counted in minutes, he knew that the truck wouldn't be able to pass this obstacle.

"What now, Dad? I guess we get to go back?"

Jeff took a deep breath and then exhaled just as deeply. "Yes. We can't cross the median here, because of the concrete barriers, and trying to drive the wrong way on the other side would be suicide."

"I guess I should turn around." As soon as he said it, Robbie realized how dumb his statement sounded. At the same time, the idea of driving the wrong way on the highway seemed weird.

Jeff was also trying to make sense of their situation. It took him a couple seconds longer than it normally would to respond. "Yeah, we need to turn around quickly, before someone else shows up. The last thing we need now is to have cars backing up behind us. Put it in reverse, back up toward the shoulder over there, and start driving back."

With Jeff's mostly unneeded guidance, Robbie turned the wheel hard, backed toward the side of the highway, then turned the wheel hard the other direction and drove forward again, this time headed east, back toward the east side of North Bend.

Robbie accelerated down I-90, in the wrong direction.

"Get on the far left shoulder," Jeff said. "We don't want someone running into us head-on."

No sooner than Robbie moved over to the shoulder, they saw a compact car flying by in the other direction, in the middle lane. It slowed down slightly as it passed them. Robbie honked his horn, trying to alert the man to the problem that waited for him around the bend, but the man only gawked at them, then increased speed again, driving unknowingly toward the landslide.

"Well, you tried," Jeff said. "Take the next exit. We have to go through town. We'll be exiting the wrong way, but there should be enough room to avoid a collision if someone is exiting onto the highway. Take it slow and we'll be fine. I think we'll be able to drive back through town, go around the landslide, and get on the highway on the other side.

"Let's see if I can warn anyone. Jeff fished a compact repeater guide from the glove box. It was the *ARRL Repeater Directory*[39], and it was jam-packed with repeater listings for the entire US, which made it handy for travelling. It listed repeaters by area, including the frequencies, offset, tone, power rating, and other information. He quickly flipped to the Washington State section and found the North Bend area. He picked out what he thought might be a frequently-used repeater for the area, turned to the correct frequency, and programmed the other necessary settings. Pressing the transmit key on the radio, he asked, "This is NM8J, doing a signal check. Can anyone hear me?"

There was no reply, and even more disconcerting, there was no telltale beep that would have indicated the repeater had received his transmission and was functioning correctly. Jeff tried again. No beep, no reply. This repeater, like the others he'd tried after the quake, was not working.

Jeff pressed a button and turned a dial on the radio. "I'm going to change the frequency to the repeater's output frequency. That way anyone who is scanning for that frequency within range of our radio will hear me transmit. Soon enough, people will realize that they need to transmit on the same frequency because the repeater is down."

"This is NM8J with emergency traffic," Jeff called into the radio, after listening for a moment. "I think the repeater is down, and I'm transmitting only on the repeater's output frequency. If you're listening, you need to know that the highway headed westbound is completely blocked by a landslide about a half mile past Exit 31. If anyone can hear me, please reply by transmitting on this same frequency. Again, the repeater is down. Please reply by transmitting on this same frequency, 145.110 megahertz."

Jeff stopped and listened. There was no response. He transmitted the message again.

Robbie approached the exit that they'd passed just a few minutes earlier and turned onto the ramp. Apparently, nobody wanted to leave town and head toward the big city, which was fine with him. He didn't feel like dodging traffic after what they'd been through already today.

Jeff sighed, wondering if anyone in the area had a working ham radio. He looked over at Robbie. "You're still doing better than me on my first driving adventure," he said with a smile.

Robbie beamed at the compliment. He felt bad about driving slowly, because he wanted to get them home as quickly as possible. At the same time, he knew he didn't have a choice. His dad's support helped.

The radio squawked, catching them both by surprise. "NM8J this is KD9PW. I received your message. I had to change my transmit frequency, and it took a few seconds."

"OK," Jeff replied. "You got my message, right? The highway is completely blocked westbound."

"Yes, received, I-90 blocked westbound, just west of exit 31."

"Correct. What's your name? I'm Jeff."

"I'm Larry. That was some quake."

"Listen Larry," Jeff started, with a tone that indicated there was no time for small-talk. "We need to let people know about this[40]. There may not be a lot of people headed back into Seattle, but if you don't want to see a traffic jam out here, and a bunch of refugees who run out of gas and evacuate into North Bend, you should see if you can get someone to put up detour signs before exit 31. We just took that exit — it's the only way to continue westward. They'll need to exit there and drive through town in order to get back on the highway."

"Well, I'm not sure that's going to happen anytime soon. It's a real a mess here. And your assumption may be wrong. They might not be able to drive through town either."

As Robbie continued toward the end of the exit ramp and they got a better view of North Bend, they realized what Larry was talking about. About half of the visible buildings were on fire.

26. Navigating the Wreckage

Robbie pulled to the shoulder and stopped. He and Jeff stared ahead in fascinated horror.

When the earthquake struck, most of the damage was centered in the Seattle area. Since Seattle was unfortunately built directly on a fault line, much of the destruction was catastrophic. But even 30 miles away in North Bend, due to the size and ferocity of the quake, the damaging effects were severe. The combination of the incredible shaking, even at this distance from the epicenter, and the construction practices at the time when the natural gas lines were installed in North Bend, led to several critical failures. On the northeast side of town, one intersection of two major gas lines was completely severed as pipes were simply pulled apart. In two other places, as the pipeline bisected the town from east to west, the line cracked enough to quickly release all of the pressurized natural gas in the lines.

Maybe because of pilot lights in water heaters and gas stoves, electrical wires short-circuiting, or maybe even because of a burning cigarette falling out of the mouth of someone standing slack-jawed, watching buildings collapse, two large fires had started. Initially fueled by natural gas, and later fueled further by wood buildings it consumed as it grew, the fire roared through the already-devastated southern part of town.

From their vantage point, Robbie and Jeff could see three North Bend fire engines parked in one area, with nearby firefighters directing water onto two buildings not yet completely engulfed in flames.

As they watched, one of the hoses stopped spraying water. One of the engines had probably exhausted the onboard water tank. Jeff wondered how long the other two would last.

"Larry, I can see that much of the town is on fire. And the part that's not on fire appears to be severely damaged from the quake. Where are you? Are you OK?"

Jeff didn't really think they'd have any time or ability to help Larry even if he wasn't OK, but fell back on his polite habits and had to ask. He was hoping that Larry could continue to operate his radio and help keep locals informed and relay emergency messages.

"I'm OK. I'm up on the hill to the south, on the other side of the highway. I can see into town, but my house is OK. I had it earthquake-proofed a few years ago. In fact, the guy..."

Jeff knew that Larry was shaken up and wanted to talk. But they had no time. He set the handset in his lap as he turned to Robbie.

"We have to get through here soon, before the fire spreads or something else happens. Drive up to the intersection and take a left. Go slowly. The last thing we need now is a wreck. Our goal is to get to the other side of town, where we'll find the next off-ramp, so we can get back on I-90."

"Got it, Dad," Robbie replied with confidence.

Larry stopped talking for a moment. Jeff took the opportunity to speak before Larry started up again.

"Larry, listen, this is important. You may be the only guy in the area who can warn people. You should probably keep transmitting on this frequency. If anyone is scanning repeater frequencies, they'll hear you sooner or later. Everyone who's heading westbound needs to know that the road is blocked."

Jeff thought for a moment. Before Larry could answer, he spoke again. "Do you have an ARES or RACES[41] group in North Bend, as far as you know?"

Larry had started to come out of his shock, and was ready to get down to business. "I have a flyer around here somewhere. I think they have a weekly radio net[42]. I remember writing down that frequency somewhere."

"Get on that frequency too, and let them know. Hopefully many of them have backup power and working radios. They should be prepared for a power outage, and will know who to sync up with. Let them know about the blocked road too, so they can relay that information."

"Larry," Jeff said slowly and seriously, "it's up to you now to get the word out. Do you have enough power to keep transmitting for a while?"

"Yeah," Larry replied, sounding serious now too. "My power is still on. One of my neighbors said that a block over, the power is out, but at least on my block we still have power. And if it goes out, I have a generator and some backup batteries to run my radio. I'm topping off the charge on them right now, just in case."

"Sounds like a good idea. Use the power while you have it. Now I have to go. We have to get back to Bellevue. It's all up to you now. Make sure people in the area know what's going on. Good luck."

"Thanks Jeff. Good luck to you."

"NM8J clear and monitoring."

"KD9PW clear and monitoring." Larry was already sounding in control of the situation.

Robbie drove slowly down a main road, headed west, carefully weaving around occasional pieces of debris in the roadway. He stayed clear of the few other, slowly-moving cars on the road. Now the road curved to the north, toward the fire. He pulled over to the shoulder and stopped again.

"What now, Dad? The road looks like it's taking us toward the fire."

"Up there — see the left turn we can take?" Jeff pointed to a side road about twenty yards ahead. "Let's turn there."

Robbie pulled out onto the road again. They heard the screech of brakes and a blaring horn as a car swerved around them, also heading north.

"Dang it!" Robbie said, shaking his head. They couldn't afford any stupid mistakes, and he'd just made one.

"Yeah, you probably should have looked before pulling onto the roadway. And I should have looked too. That was my fault. Sorry, Robbie. Lesson learned. You're doing great though. Just keep going."

Jeff felt bad about not having time to be thorough in Robbie's driver training. It was obviously a ridiculous environment for a driver's education course, but he was doing his best, and they didn't really have a choice.

Robbie carefully took the left-hand turn into a neighborhood, hoping it had an exit to the main road that led to the next I-90 onramp.

"Hold on!" Jeff said excitedly.

Robbie slowed down even further, unsure of what Jeff was asking.

"No, sorry, keep going. I just remembered. Even though the phones don't work, the GPS still does!" Jeff had become accustomed to using the GPS functionality in his cell phone. When the phones stopped working, he had been too distracted to think about switching to another device. And since they had known exactly where they were going until just recently, they hadn't needed to think about any alternative.

Jeff pulled a GPS unit from the glove compartment. He plugged the charger into the 12-volt outlet in the dashboard and turned it on.

"Give it a minute to lock onto some satellites, and we'll be in business," Jeff said. "In fact, you might as well pull over for a minute while we figure it out, in case we're going the wrong way right now."

Robbie pulled over and looked at the GPS with Jeff, watching an hourglass symbol spin around slowly as the GPS receiver locked on to several satellites and triangulated the truck's position. About a minute later, a map appeared. Jeff zoomed in, so that they could get a better view of the city and this neighborhood.

"Look," Jeff said. "We can follow this road to the main road, and get back on the highway here." He pointed to the road that ran north-south, almost parallel to Interstate-90. They would be able to get onto that road as soon as they got out of this neighborhood. Luckily, they had been going the right direction.

"OK, I'll keep going the same way," Robbie said, as he pulled back onto the road and drove north, into the heart of the neighborhood.

Whether because of building code standards, earthquake retrofitting, or just because of dumb luck, some houses were standing and appeared to be untouched by the quake, while others had fully or partially collapsed. Robbie remembered a video about tornados they'd watched once in his Earth Science class at school. They had seen where a tornado had come through and totally destroyed some houses, while leaving some others undamaged only a few dozen yards away. The path of devastation in this neighborhood wasn't as clear as the path of destruction the tornado left behind, but there were still clusters of houses standing near areas where many houses had collapsed.

As they slowly passed one collapsed house, they saw several people standing outside, shouting at the house. Apparently someone was trapped inside. A woman sat outside on the sidewalk, her hands on her face, crying uncontrollably, with another man sitting next to her, his face showing his own pain as he tried to comfort her. Two other men were wedging a board under part of a partially collapsed wall, to keep it from collapsing further, and several other people stood and watched with helpless expressions on their faces.

"Dad, can we help them?"

Jeff was quiet. Robbie slowed down even more.

A few people outside the house looked their way, but did nothing.

Jeff said "Keep going. They have it under control, and we have to get back to our house."

Jeff didn't need to say that their house could also have collapsed.

"See the green vest that guy is wearing?" He pointed to one of the men trying to wedge the board under a leaning wall. "That's a CERT vest. He must have taken the CERT training, which means he has at least very basic training about what to do. That's probably as good as they're going to get for a while."

Robbie felt his eyes fill with tears as he continued driving. He imagined a similar scene at his home, and thought about how it would be if his mom and Lisa were trapped inside.

The people outside the house turned back to their work as Robbie accelerated and drove away.

Robbie and Jeff saw similar scenes several more times, people in clusters outside fallen houses, some trying to get inside, some just watching. Robbie and Jeff would occasionally wave somberly as they passed, but most of the time, as soon as people noticed that they weren't firefighters or police officers, they turned their attention back to their destroyed homes or trapped neighbors.

Robbie and Jeff continued to drive slowly through the neighborhood, occasionally driving around debris that had spilled into the roadway. They eventually neared the edge of the neighborhood. They saw the highway only a hundred yards away, through the gap between two lightly-damaged houses.

"Look Dad — we're close!" Robbie said excitedly.

"Almost there!" Jeff said.

Robbie slammed on the brakes again.

This time he was faster than his father. Jeff had been thinking about the highway and trying to figure out what road led to the highway on-ramp. Robbie had been looking forward for about a second before Jeff had turned his attention back to the road. During that second Robbie couldn't help but notice the spray of sparks that shot out from a long, black snake lying in the roadway. A snapped power line was lying across the road, waiting for them, directly in their path. If the sparks hadn't alerted him, Robbie may not have seen it.

"You're turning into a good driver," Jeff said. "You're doing a great job paying attention to the road."

Robbie beamed.

It was true. Robbie's driving skills had improved since earlier in the afternoon. Of course, anyone could reasonably argue that they could only improve when starting with no skills at all, aside from those learned playing video games. However, Robbie had a knack for problem-solving. Much of the challenge of driving, whether it's getting along with the other vehicles on the road, timing turns appropriately, or navigating both unexpected obstacles, is related to problem-solving abilities. So even though Robbie hadn't spent any time on the road driving a real car or truck, this ability started to reveal itself in new ways. In this case, with the sparks alerting him to take action, braking was almost instinctual, one of the easiest problems to solve so far today: see sparks, stop the truck.

For a few seconds after the truck screeched to a halt, Robbie and Jeff sat and stared at the scene in front of them. They could see that the fallen power line draped across a parked car and then crossed the road. There was no way to drive down the road without touching the line. Even though power appeared to be out in many areas, it appeared to be on here, which meant that this wire could kill them both in an instant.

Robbie looked left, looked right, and spoke. "I don't want to touch that wire, and I don't want to go back. Maybe we can go around it. That yard on the right looks like a safe way to go."

"You're right. We can't drive over that power line," Jeff replied. "Even though we're insulated from the ground because of our tires, it's a bad idea." He looked around a little bit more. Robbie had assessed the situation correctly. "You're right. That yard on the right looks clear, and we'll be able to keep at least two wheels on the sidewalk, so we should have no problem. Put it into four-wheel drive and go slowly."

Robbie pressed a button on the dashboard, and the truck shifted into four-wheel-drive, then turned the steering wheel sharply to the right and gently pressed down on the accelerator. The truck crawled over the curb, onto the sidewalk. Robbie steered toward the lawn, intending to use the sidewalk and part of the lawn as their new path. As they neared the far edge of the lawn, the front door of the nearby house door popped open and a man jumped out, wearing a dingy, white bathrobe. He was fat, and the robe barely fit around his midsection. But despite his size, he moved quickly, and he appeared to be angry.

"What the heck are you doing? Get off of my lawn! I'm calling the cops!"

Startled, but not slowing down, Robbie continued to drive carefully.

"Sorry — we need to get to the highway," Jeff called back, through the partially-opened passenger side window.

A second later, Robbie turned the wheel sharply to the left, dropped down off of the sidewalk, and they were back on the road. They could hear the man shouting curses at them, enraged at the shallow track their passenger side tires had left in his lawn.

As they continued down the road, Robbie glanced in the rearview mirror. The man was still in the yard, yelling at them.

"Wow," Robbie said. "It's like he didn't even realize there was an earthquake. He's worried about his lawn!"

"I bet we'll see more unusual behavior before the day is over," Jeff replied.

27. Breaking In

After breaking the window, Luis reached up and broke away some large, remaining pieces of glass. Cursing, he snatched his hand back — he'd cut his palm on a sharp shard. Now there was blood on his palm and it was getting everywhere. It wasn't a very serious cut, and while it hurt, Luis was concerned for another reason. He knew that blood was evidence. He remembered the story he'd heard from one of the guys he played cards with in prison. The man had been caught because of several of drops of blood he'd left at the scene of a homicide, and now he got to spend at least another decade in prison before being considered for parole. The man had protested his innocence and repeatedly told Luis that he'd been framed, but that didn't stop Luis from continuing his education. He learned that leaving your blood at the scene of a crime was a bad idea. And now he wondered how he was going to clean this up.

Then Luis remembered — there were no cops now! He could do whatever he wanted. Luis didn't need to act "normal" any more, or pretend to be a "good citizen", or even worry about evidence or witnesses or anything else. He could take what he wanted from this house and move on, and nobody could do anything about it, whether his blood was here or not.

By this time Luis was cut, tired, thirsty, and starting to get angry. He brushed away the remaining shards of glass, more carefully this time. With blood trickling down his arm and a dull, throbbing pain in his hand from the cut, he pushed the curtain aside.

After opening the door to the garage, Marie looked for the source of the breaking glass sound. She didn't see anything unusual, or any broken glass on the floor. Aside from the window behind the shelving unit and some canned food on the pantry shelf, she didn't remember anything made of glass in the garage. She double-checked the pantry shelf. Although some metal cans had fallen to the floor from the front row, the home-canned fruit and vegetables in their glass jars had been toward the back, and they hadn't fallen.

Wondering what she'd heard, her attention jumped to a sound on the far side of the garage. It was more breaking glass, and now she knew where it was coming from. Something moved behind the shelves. There was a window on that far wall, and she had covered it with curtains before putting the metal shelving in place. Leaving the window exposed and accessible would have sacrificed too much storage space, so they'd just covered it with a curtain, to let in some light during the day and simultaneously keep prying eyes out. As she looked closer, between two boxes on the shelf, she saw the curtain move, and then saw a bloody hand reach in and brush the curtain aside.

Instinctively, Marie stepped back into the hallway and closed the door. In her alarm, she almost slammed the door, but at the last moment, she slowed down and left the door opened a crack. Her first thought had been to run away, but she immediately realized that she needed to know what she was up against. She didn't want to risk being seen by the intruder, but she knew that it would be difficult for someone to see her. Since there was no power, the hallway behind her was dark, so she was effectively hidden in the shadows.

A second later, she watched as her fears were confirmed. Between the boxes, she caught a flash of an angry, unshaven face with narrow-set eyes and dark, messy hair. She'd never seen the man before. He stuck his head partially through the window and looked around at the boxes and shelving in front of it. Then she heard him curse angrily.

As quickly and quietly as she could, Marie shut the door and locked it. She never expected that someone would try to break into their house, especially right after an earthquake. This was unbelievable. They had just survived a huge earthquake, and now someone was trying to break into their house. Thank God he had chosen the wrong window. He'd never get past the shelving and boxes. Not quickly, anyway.

Now that Marie knew what was happening, she came up with a quick plan. She and Lisa would get out of the house, through the front door. The man was probably going to try to break in somewhere through the back. She rushed back down the hall and hissed "Lisa — we need to go! Come here now!"

There was no scampering of feet, only silence.

Lisa wasn't in the kitchen. And she wasn't in the living room. The front door was still closed, and Marie felt a sinking feeling in her stomach. Lisa was probably somewhere upstairs.

Marie rushed up the stairs and to Lisa's bedroom. She threw open the door. It was empty. She ran down to the end of the hall, to the master bedroom. She opened door, mentally crossing her fingers. Lisa sat in the middle of the bedroom floor, talking to her Teddy bear.

"Mommy, Teddy was afraid. I'm taking care of him."

"Lisa — get up and come with me right now. We need to go outside." She tried to sound calm, but more than anything, she wanted to run out of the house.

Lisa got up, wondering what was wrong.

Luis looked through the curtain he had pushed aside and cursed angrily. This window didn't provide an entrance to the garage. It was almost completely blocked by a shelf that cut off the bottom third of the window. And the boxes sitting on that shelf were big, and probably heavy. But it didn't matter. He couldn't fit through here.

To make matters worse, between curses, he heard the "*snick*" of a door lock being turned. The lady must have seen him, and now she had locked the door to the garage. This was getting more and more annoying.

But he wasn't ready to give up. Luis had dealt with bigger problems than this, and decided that since she already knew he was here, there was no use trying to be sneaky. It was time to take a more direct approach, get what he wanted here, and move on.

He picked up another rock from the ground as he walked around the back of the house, up to the French doors he had peered through earlier, and threw the rock through the pane next to the door handle. There was no need to be quiet now. Get in, tie up the woman and kid, find the money, jewelry, and whatever else, and move on to the next house.

Marie heard a sound that chilled her blood: more breaking glass. She knew what has happened. The man had broken the glass on one of the French doors downstairs. He was in the house. She couldn't go back down the stairs with Lisa without confronting him. They were trapped.

Lisa was getting ready to go outside, but also heard the breaking glass and knew something was wrong.

"What's happening, Mommy?"

"Hush. Stay quiet. We're changing plans." Marie thought for a couple seconds and then made a decision.

"Get in the closet. Take Teddy with you."

Lisa recognized the tone in her mother's voice, and knew she meant business. She ran into the walk-in closed and poked her head out, watching Marie.

Marie thought for a second, grabbed her handheld radio from where it sat in its charger on the small table near the window, and clipped it to her belt. She shut the bedroom door and locked it. The door was lightweight and had a flimsy, interior door lock that would probably give way with a sharp kick, but hopefully it would buy her some time.

Luis quickly cleared the glass away from the door pane, more carefully this time, making sure to not cut himself again. He reached inside and turned the lock on the door. It wouldn't move. He twisted harder, but it still wouldn't budge. He tried the door handle. It turned freely. The door had been unlocked all along. Cursing more loudly now, he opened the door and walked inside. This house and its inhabitants were making him more and more angry. He didn't have time for this.

Lisa ran to Marie and clutched her leg. "What's wrong Mommy?"

Marie took a precious few seconds to stand still and hug Lisa. Some of the sun's light filtered through the light curtains over the bedroom window, and in the reflection of a mirror over her dresser, she saw their reflection. They were both afraid. She and her baby girl were in danger, and she needed to act. But she didn't want to terrify her daughter. She needed to be strong.

Marie took a deep breath to calm herself. "There is a man in the house. He probably wants to take some stuff and then go away. So we're going to wait here quietly until he's done and goes away, OK?"

Lisa started to cry. "I'm afraid, Mommy."

"It's OK, baby, I'll take good care of you. Don't worry about a thing. The important thing is that we stay quiet and wait until he leaves. Your dad and brother will be back soon, and if he's still here, they'll scare him off. We just have to wait for a little while. Now get in the closet and find a comfortable place to sit. Pile up some of Mommy's folded clothes and make yourself a seat."

Lisa went back to the closet, but stood in the doorway watching, not letting Marie out of her sight.

28. Still on the Way

At Jeff's request, Robbie drove in the center lane of Interstate-90, slightly under the speed limit. They wouldn't get a ticket for exceeding the speed limit, but Jeff wanted to make sure they had enough time to see any damage in the road before they hit it. While he desperately wanted to get home, they had to stay safe.

"Dad, what's that?" Robbie asked, as he instinctively swerved to the right, into the slow lane. "That guy's going the wrong way!"

"I see it Robbie. Don't worry. Stay in this lane and keep going."

Robbie gripped the steering wheel even harder now as a full-sized, dark green pickup truck sped by in the far left lane, going the wrong way. They saw the driver for an instant as he passed them, and he didn't even look over at them. He had both hands on the wheel, and was staring straight ahead. The tailgate was down. Evidently he hadn't even taken the time to shut it before taking off. Jeff turned back and saw that the truck bed was completely empty. He had no extra gas cans or supplies.

"I wonder how far he'll get?" said Jeff. "If the pass is blocked he's going to be a refugee up there."

Before Jeff could say anything else, another vehicle sped toward them. This one was a station wagon. As it passed, they could see that it was packed to the roof with luggage and other stuff, and there was a child in the back seat. Two large, cardboard boxes were tied haphazardly to the roof rack with rope. The ends of the rope fluttered as they sped by.

As Robbie and Jeff continued toward Bellevue, an occasional car passed them the wrong way, driving eastbound in the westbound lanes. Before long, light traffic grew into a steady stream. Most of the drivers stayed in the fast lane, their instincts apparently still telling them that even in this unusual situation, going the wrong way was dangerous and they should keep to the left side of the road as much as possible. Even so, traffic increased and started to fill the middle lane too. Jeff and Robbie were quickly running out of highway.

With no other choice now, Robbie continued to drive in the slow lane, ready to drive onto the shoulder at any moment. Jeff had turned on their emergency blinkers a few minutes ago, and showed Robbie how to flash the headlight high beams whenever he saw another car coming in the middle lane.

As they drove closer to Bellevue city limits and passed more and more houses and buildings visible from the highway, it was easy to see different kinds of damage. In the last several miles, they had seen three different fires, big ones that had engulfed several buildings. But they didn't see a single set of fire department flashing lights. They saw some collapsed and partially-collapsed buildings, with crowds of people standing around outside the rubble, huddling together in the cool air. Robbie kept driving. He kept both hands on the wheel and continued to flash his high beams whenever he saw someone approaching. Mile after mile, they continued.

"Let's try to reach your mother again," said Jeff. "Maybe we can reach home now."

Jeff picked up the radio and switched to the Mike and Key[43] repeater, which they used most often when in the Seattle area. "KD7KFT, this is NM8J, can you read me?"

There was no beep. This repeater was also off-line.

"The repeater must be down. I'll switch to our main simplex frequency," Jeff said.

Robbie continued to drive, staring straight ahead as he made white-knuckled corrections to the truck's path. Cars, trucks, station wagons, and even occasional motorcycles (with riders usually wearing large backpacks) continued to pass them in the opposite direction.

Jeff changed the channel on the radio until it said "Primary 2M Home", and called again for Marie. "KD7KFT, this is NM8J, can you hear me?" They waited. The radio was silent. They kept driving toward Bellevue at an even 50 miles per hour, emergency lights flashing. In two more exits, they would be home.

They approached Exit 13 and saw something new. They looked more closely as they passed the exit. Though the off-ramp wasn't elevated, it had still been damaged. A large crack, over a foot wide in places, stretched across the pavement that ran parallel to the highway. If they had taken the exit, they might have been able to cross the crack, but not without putting down some boards or finding another way to improvise a bridge. Hitting the crack at 50 miles per hour would have probably been disastrous, though.

"You should probably slow down a bit," Jeff said. "We might find a crack in our path, and if we do we want plenty of time to stop."

Robbie slowed down to 35 miles per hour. And they would need the extra reaction time.

Less than a mile later, Robbie had enough time to see large chunks of concrete sitting in the road. A footbridge crossed over the highway. It hadn't collapsed, but it was obviously damaged in places. Several large pieces of concrete had fallen from the cracked underside. Robbie and Jeff held their breath as

Robbie crossed under the bridge, swerving gently to the left, then to the right, to avoid the obstacles.

As they cleared the bridge, they both exhaled. Nothing had fallen on them. Robbie kept driving.

About a mile ahead, the off-ramp to 148th Avenue waited for them. And 148th[th] would take them home.

29. All the Way In

Luis looked around. There was no sign of the woman or the girl. He walked into the kitchen, where he saw several pots and pans sitting on the countertop, all filled with water. He picked up a small pan and drank from it, slopping about a quarter of it onto the front of his shirt. Then he opened the refrigerator. He figured that he had plenty of time. The woman and girl were probably hiding upstairs. He imagined them huddled in terror, hiding from the scary, bloody man who had invaded their safe place. He had nothing to worry about.

The refrigerator light didn't come on. He remembered that the power was out and cursed. He peered more closely. Among the containers and plastic bags, he spotted a see-through container that contained half a sandwich. He removed the container, took the lid off, gave the sandwich a sniff, and promptly stuffed most of it into his mouth. After another large bite and a few more chews, it was gone. He washed it down with more water. That was a lot better. It was time to get back to work, and put his hands on some valuables, maybe even a gun or a big wad of cash. Oh yeah — and the car keys, for his grand exit.

Marie retrieved a key from its hiding spot near the bed, went to the locked box bolted to the bookcase[44], opened it and retrieved a Springfield XD 9mm handgun. She stuffed it into the front of her waistband, and did a quick double-check of the bedroom. Prepared as she could be, she quickly crossed the bedroom, motioned for Lisa to go toward the back of the closet, then followed her into the closet and shut the door behind her. With no windows and no power to turn on the ceiling light, it was pitch black.

In her haste to get herself and Lisa to a safe place, Marie didn't remember the radio she had clipped to her belt, and therefore didn't remember to turn it on. She huddled in the dark with Lisa, completely cut off from the outside world.

30. Off-ramp

There was only one exit to go. Robbie and Jeff passed the exit for 161st Avenue Northeast, and saw that it was completely blocked by a semi-trailer which lay on its side in the road. When they looked more closely, they could see that a small section of pavement had risen up, a line that stretched from one side of the road to the other, and it looked like the semi had hit it straight on, as it exited. With the momentum of the large trailer full of whatever it was carrying to propel it forward, it simply jackknifed and flipped over. Thankfully, there was no fire. But that exit was no longer an option.

A hundred yards later, they approached the exit for 148th Avenue Northeast. Robbie slowed down to about thirty miles per hour and took the curving off-ramp that led north, toward their neighborhood.

Jeff continued to coach. "Slower. Not too fast on this curve." Robbie was driving at about 20 miles per hour now, for good reason. This intersection, where 148th intersected with I-90, was full of elevated overpasses, on-ramps, and off-ramps. There was a good chance that one or more of the elevated sections of road had collapsed partially or completely, and in either case, the area could be treacherous.

As they rounded the bend, they could see about 30 yards ahead. Cars were parked on all the roads they could see. Robbie slowed to a crawl as they took in the incredible mass of traffic.

This was unexpected good news. The roads here were all intact. Whether it was because of recent seismic retrofitting, underlying geology that made the area exceptionally stable, or just luck, all of the roads were in one piece. And this meant that this was one of the few places where someone could get on the highway, and all of these people appeared to know it.

"Wow. We thought the highway was bad. This area is even worse," Jeff said.

"Maybe it's because they all want to get onto the highway to get out of here," Robbie replied.

"Yeah. I think you're right. Pull onto the shoulder for a minute."

Robbie pulled onto the shoulder. No other vehicles were exiting in their direction at the moment. They appeared to be safe from any speeding traffic. As they sat and watched for a minute, the scene ahead worsened. They watched, fascinated by the chaos.

Traffic stretched in all directions. Traffic lights weren't working, which added to the mess. When a rare chance to move forward came up, most people took turns, but some people were too panicked and as soon as they reached an intersection, they just drove through, even if someone else was trying to cross at the same time. This resulted in even worse slow-downs as mini-jams had to be resolved at each intersection.

People waiting in traffic were quickly running out of patience and many had started to honk their horns. This made some people feel better. It was one of the few things they could control in this crazy situation. But others took the honking personally and chose to get angry.

Robbie and Jeff sat watching, looking for any possible way to get past this latest obstacle.

As they watched, they saw something unusual in the middle of the main roadway ahead, near the intersection where traffic was thickest. A tough-looking man got out of his dark green pickup truck, walked to a blue Toyota sedan behind his, which was still honking, and gave the door a fierce kick and shouted angrily. Even from the distance, Robbie and Jeff could tell the man was enraged — his face was red and his movements were aggressive. He shouted and kicked the door again. Then to their surprise, he punched the driver-side window. It shattered.

They could see the driver of the Toyota frantically crawling over to the passenger side of the car, as the angry man reached inside the window. He continued to shout. Then the attacker opened the driver side door and started to climb inside. The passenger door flew open but nobody came out. Jeff and Robbie saw a tangle of moving limbs inside, and a second later a shot rang out.

The sound was incredibly loud. Most of the honking stopped as startled drivers looked around to see what had happened, trying to determine whether more shots were coming, or whether they were in danger.

The attacker, now more confused than angry, pushed himself out of the driver side onto the pavement and fell to the ground, holding one hand over his other arm, where a patch of blood stood out against the arm of his white t-shirt.

Then the driver of the Toyota fell out of the passenger side, landing on his back on the pavement. He stood up quickly and regained his balance. He quickly backed away from his car, and then Robbie and Jeff saw he was holding a pistol in his hand. Two men who had been approaching the scene from a couple car-lengths back, whether to try to break it up or to join in the fight, saw it too and decided that they didn't need to be involved any further. They spun around immediately and ran back to their cars. A few people screamed and several panicked drivers tried to drive away from the dangerous scene.

The honking started up again, this time with a much more urgent quality than before. Unfortunately, two of the most panicked drivers immediately crashed into nearby cars in their hopeless attempt to flee. Since there was nowhere to go, all that these drivers succeeded in doing was turning the traffic jam into a hopeless deadlock.

Robbie and Jeff sat in the truck in shock[45]. Jeff blinked his eyes and shook his head. This was not a good place to be, and they had already wasted precious seconds watching the horrifying events unfold. Of course, he was surprised to see such violence, but he was even more surprised at how the situation had gotten so bad in such a short amount of time.

Robbie had also realized they needed to move. "How are we going to get home? We have to get past that!" he said with a tremor in his voice. He was hunched down slightly in his seat, after instinctively ducking seconds ago.

"We can't go that way. There's a wall of cars up there. They're all stuck, and they don't even know how bad it is on the highway. And there's at least one man with a gun. This is really bad. We have to get out of here and try something else."

"Then how will we get home?"

"We have to take a different way. If we get stuck down there, we'll be hiking home, and it's looking more and more dangerous on the street."

Suddenly, a car sped past them, down the ramp, and directly into the snarled traffic. The driver was obviously in such a hurry that he didn't take the time to look ahead, at the trap he was driving into. Robbie and Jeff watched as the car quickly added to the deadlock.

"Put the truck in reverse and lightly step on the gas," Jeff said. "Make sure you go slowly. It's easy to mess up when driving backwards. If you get confused, just hit the brakes and try again."

Robbie drove as instructed. About halfway up the ramp, he turned the steering wheel to adjust for the curve of the road and nearly drove into the ditch. He quickly stepped on the brakes.

"Good job," Jeff said. "You kept us out of the ditch. Now turn the wheels the other way and get back on the road."

"That was close. I got a little mixed up," Robbie said. "It's backwards." He felt dumb for saying the words.

"Yeah, don't worry about it. You're getting the hang of it just fine. You're a smart kid. I didn't learn to drive nearly as quickly as you did."

"I'm not a kid. Look at me — I'm driving a truck. And I rescued you today."

"Sorry son. You're right. How about we say 'young man'?"

"That'll be OK for now," Robbie said. He straightened the wheels and continued backing up.

"Stop when you get to the highway. Let's make sure nobody is trying to crash into us." Robbie stopped near the intersection with the highway. Luckily, the traffic going the wrong way in their lane was still pretty light.

"Now turn around and we'll find a way off the highway while we're driving away from the city. Now we'll be driving the wrong way too…"

Jeff talked Robbie through a simple three-point turn so they could also drive eastward.

"Good job," Jeff said, with pride in his voice. "You'll be ready to pass your driving test soon."

Robbie grinned up at his father. "Thanks Dad. What now?"

"Drive on the left shoulder here. Go slowly, in case we get someone driving the right direction on the road. By the way, don't do this on your driver's test."

Robbie rolled his eyes. "OK Dad." The drove slowly, 100 meters, 200 meters. The exit ramp fell into the distance behind them. They passed the flipped-over semi on their left, and kept going.

Jeff leaned over toward the steering wheel and pulled a key off of the clip that secured it to the key ring. Then he leaned back between the seats, and reached over to the floor of the cab.

"I should have thought of this earlier. That crazy man back there caught me by surprise."

He unlocked a flat metal box that was secured to the steel frame of the passenger seat with a steel cable. Robbie watched sideways with wide eyes as Jeff pulled out a small handgun in a leather holster, and then picked up a spare magazine that had been stored with it. He sat back down in his seat, clipped the holster to his waistband, and stuck the spare magazine in his pocket.

Robbie tried to focus on driving, but kept glancing over at Jeff as he secured the handgun.

"Don't worry," Jeff said. "If we're smart, we'll have no need for this. The last thing I want to do is take this out and use it. But you saw what happened back there. I don't want someone going crazy on us. I have to protect you."

Robbie thought about how serious things had become. Earlier in the day he'd been thinking about playing video games, and now he was wondering if the next turn would bring a life-or-death problem they'd have to solve.

"Up there ahead!" Jeff said. "Do you see that spot where the ditch levels out? We're going to cross there. Slow down now.... slow... and stop." They sat at a place where the shoulder on their left side was relatively flat, and they could see a surface street only about 30 meters away. But there was a chain-link fence in the way.

"How do we get through the fence, Dad?"

Jeff reached over and turned on the emergency lights. "If you see anyone coming, flash the high beams. Make sure they don't hit you." He thought for a second. "No, I changed my mind. People are losing their minds, so you'll be better off with me. We'll leave the truck there with the headlights on. Help me get the fence out of our way. I have some wire cutters back here. They should do the trick." Jeff opened the passenger door and gingerly stepped out, favoring his injured ankle. He opened the back door to the extended cab and fished around in a small toolbox he'd pulled from under the back bench. He emerged with a pair of heavy-duty wire cutters, which he stuck into his belt. He picked up his improvised crutch. "Come on."

Robbie followed as Jeff hobbled over to the fence and started snipping the wire from top to bottom, link by link. He stopped before he reached the bottom, leaving two links attached. It looked like there was just enough room between two of the fence poles for the truck to fit, once the fence was out of the way. Jeff moved to the near side of the next fence pole to the left and started snipping again.

Robbie looked up and saw a car bearing down on the truck in the fast lane. The car wasn't driving on the shoulder, but it would still be close! Robbie watched as the car swerved toward the center lane at the last second and sped by.

Jeff was done cutting the links on the other side now. He pushed the length of fence down to the ground. It was still attached at the bottom on both sides, but its weight kept it lying flat, facing away from the highway. They both went back to the truck and got in.

"Why did you fold the fence down?" Robbie asked.

"The ground looked soft on the other side. The fence on the ground will give us extra traction and will hopefully keep us from getting stuck. Now let's go. I want you to drive at about 20 miles per hour. It will probably feel fast, but we want to have momentum when we drive through the soft area on this side. We don't want to get stuck. It's not too soft on this side, but I don't want to chance it. Drive straight through the opening in the fence, and don't stop until you get to the shoulder of the street over there. Then we'll be on solid ground again."

Robbie looked at the gap in the fence. "Will we fit?"

"I think so," Jeff replied. "If not, we may lose a side mirror. Hold on — roll down the window and fold them back, just in case." They folded the mirrors inward, so they were flush with the side of the truck. They still stuck out a few inches, but less than before. "OK, ready. Start fast, but don't go over 20. And stop when you're on the shoulder of the road on the other side."

Robbie turned the wheel and stepped on the gas. They accelerated as he turned the wheels to aim the truck through the gap in the fence. They lurched and bounced forward as they drove over the uneven ground. Robbie concentrated as much as he could, glancing down at the speedometer only once. They were going just under 20 MPH.

He gripped the wheel tightly with both hands, concentrated intently on the hole in the fence, and guided the large truck toward the center. The truck lurched over a bump, and Robbie lost control of the wheel for a fraction of a second. They were off-center, and instead of aiming at the opening, they were heading directly toward the right fence pole.

31. Exit Plan B

Robbie inhaled sharply and turned the steering wheel hard to the left. He overcorrected, and now they were aiming too far left. In the last fraction of a second, he turned the wheel back toward the right, not as hard this time. With a horrible screech of metal on metal, they scraped through the gap.

Robbie cringed but didn't stop. He kept pressure on the accelerator and drove over the chain-link fence without slowing down. As soon as the front wheels drove over the far edge of the fencing, he felt the front end sink slightly in the soft dirt. But because of his speed, there was enough momentum to keep them going. The rear wheels cleared the fence and three seconds later, the truck pulled up onto the solid shoulder of the smaller, neighborhood street. Robbie stopped the truck and put the transmission into park. He was panting. He had been holding his breath the whole time.

"Did I break anything?" Robbie asked.

"Wait for a minute, and stay alert," Jeff said. "I'll take a look, and then I'm going to fix the fence. Honk if you're worried about anything. This should only take a few seconds." Jeff opened the back door of the cab again, and looked around on the floor, then stuck something in his back pocket. He hobbled around the truck, inspecting the damage from the scrape with the fence. He gave Robbie a "thumbs-up", then crutched his way over to the fence. When he reached the fence, he balanced on one leg and lifted the flattened section until it was vertical again. Holding the center in place with one hand, he grabbed his crutch and pushed the end into the dirt, then propped it into the fencing on the right side. This kept the fence upright as Jeff pulled out two zip-ties[46] and reattached the top of the fence on the left side, then the right. He attached two more in the middle, one on each side. When was done, it was difficult to notice that the fence had been cut at all. It almost looked as good as new. Jeff retrieved his crutch and hobbled back to the truck.

"Why did you do that Dad?"

"Well, there's a chance that we may need to come or go again, and if we leave this open, I guarantee you that someone will take their car and get stuck, blocking the way. Now we have a private back-door to the highway."

"Cool. It's a secret highway on-ramp that goes the wrong way. I always wanted one of those," Robbie said grinning.

"Who wouldn't want one of those?" Jeff answered, grinning back. Then his expression turned serious again. The light-hearted moment was over. "Now let's get home. We better call your mom. I know she's worried about us."

Jeff pressed the transmit button on the radio. "KD7KFT, this is NM8J. Can you read me?"

There was no answer. Jeff called again. Still no answer.

"Maybe she's busy outside and doesn't have the radio turned up loud enough," Robbie said.

"Maybe," Jeff replied with a frown, clearly concerned. He called again. The radio stayed silent. They continued driving. Something was definitely wrong.

32. Cornered

Luis quickly scanned the living room. The first thing he noticed was that there were a lot of books on shelves, shelves that covered much of the side wall except for a window. Useless junk, he thought. When he saw the wood stove in the corner, he thought that the books would make good fuel for it. It looked like it hadn't been used recently. There was a plant sitting on top. The woman must have been in the process of cleaning it out; the door was open and there was a small bucket of ashes and a scoop nearby. If he decided to stay the night, he'd make sure it didn't get cold. Those books could keep this place warm for at least a few days.

As he completed his scan of the room, he saw a flat-screen TV. Probably 40 inches, he estimated. Bingo — that would get him a few bucks at his favorite local pawn shop. He could even take the lady's car to transport it. And he could probably take some other big things he hadn't thought about before. Yeah, this would work out perfectly.

That the few pawn shops in the area were either closed or destroyed because of the quake never occurred to Luis.

He kept looking. In the meantime, he unplugged the TV and hefted it over near the front door, grunting and cursing and trying not to drop it.

"KD7KFT, this is NM8J. Can you read me?"

149

Luis nearly dropped the TV in surprise. He quickly set his prize down and looked around. Who was there? He hadn't seen anyone.

"KD7KFT, this is NM8J. Are you there?"

Now he saw where the sound had come from. On the bookshelf near were the TV had been sat what looked like a fancy CB radio. It was quiet now, but it was lit up, which was odd since the power was out. Someone was obviously calling someone else. It was probably old men wanting to talk to each other about the earthquake, Luis thought. At one of the foster homes he'd live in for about a year, before getting into too much trouble with the neighborhood kids, the old man had a radio he talked on sometimes. He'd just sit there talking about the weather and his foot surgery —blah blah blah. He had tried to interest Luis in "ham radio" and tried to get him to take some tests so he could talk too, but Luis wasn't the least bit interested, and couldn't imagine any reason why he'd want to play with a radio when a cell phone or email was so much more convenient.

In any case, the radio was certainly valuable. He'd take it with him on his way out the door. He picked up the radio, disconnected the antenna cable from the back and followed the power cable, expecting it to plug into the wall. But it wasn't. It was plugged into a small, heavy battery in the back of the shelf. The battery appeared to be wired to another device, which was plugged into the wall. Luis just yanked out the wire that led to the battery, wrapped it around the radio, and set it down. Next to the radio was another device. He looked at it closely. He saw the word "Scanner" printed on the side, with some manufacturer's name and a model number. He'd heard about scanners in prison. Sometimes people would use them to listen to the cops talking on their radios. In any case, it had to be worth something too. He unplugged it and wrapped up the cord, grabbed the radio, and set them both on the floor by the doorway next to the TV. Things were looking up. This stuff would be worth good money for sure.

He finished his walk around the first floor, scanning methodically. This part of the house was done. He saw nothing else valuable. After thinking for another second, he remembered what he had seen earlier in the kitchen, and went back. He walked over to the counter next to the refrigerator, selected a long carving knife from the knife block, and stuck it in his belt. He figured it might come in handy if he needed to intimidate the woman into giving up their valuables.

Now armed and ready for anything, Luis moved toward the stairs. People always had their best stuff upstairs.

Marie fumbled around for a moment on the top shelf of the closet, and suddenly the small room was dimly illuminated. She had retrieved a small, battery-powered LED lantern from a closet shelf and turned it on. As she stood there thinking, her brow wrinkled momentarily as she realized the door wasn't fully secured, and she reached over and turned the deadbolt above the door handle.

With that task complete, Marie reached to the rear of the same shelf where she had found the lantern, and pulled down a small cardboard box. She opened it and pulled out a small foil packet, then fished around and found a small pair of scissors. The snipped off the top corner of the packet and passed it to Lisa.

"Here, take a drink, and be careful to not spill. It's full of water," Marie whispered. She thought that giving Lisa something to do would help keep her calm.

"I'm not thirsty," Lisa whispered back.

"Just try a little. It'll help you feel better. We'll be fine in here. We have water, the door is solid, and I think we even have a little food. We'll be fine until Daddy gets home, so we'll just relax and wait. Don't worry about any sounds outside. We're safe in here."

Though she put on a confident face, Marie was worried. She hadn't ever had a stranger break into her house, and never thought someone would have the nerve to do that while she was home. She looked at her hands. They were sweaty and shaking. She squeezed them into fists and took a couple deep breaths. She had to look calm for Lisa. If she wanted to prevent Lisa from becoming terrified, which could have long-term psychological effects, Marie needed to keep up the calm appearance. She thought back to an occasion when she was a child, and a time when she had been truly terrified. Looking back now, she knew that it wasn't actually a big deal. A neighbor's dog had been clipped on the backside by a passing car. While the dog's yelping was scary and made her feel sad, it was her mother's reaction that actually terrified her at the time. Marie's mother wasn't very level-headed, and she had initially screamed, and then cried for several minutes before someone was able to calm her down. It was almost as if *she* had been hit by the car. Apparently she thought the dog had been killed, even though she couldn't see it because neighbors were huddled around it. The fact that it was still yelping escaped her. In the end, the dog had only been dazed, and only an hour later it was playing with the neighbor kids again, enjoying its new lease on life. It had a limp for the next several weeks, but in the end it was fine.

Marie was aware of how her own fear could impact the girl looking up to her for support and reassurance, and she vowed she wouldn't let her fear terrify Lisa. Marie would not let this man scar her baby girl, not if there was anything in her power to prevent it.

Marie double-checked to make sure the handgun was on the top shelf where she had placed it, still within easy reach, but out of Lisa's sight.

With a forced smile on her face, Marie whispered "Let's play a word game while we wait. We'll have to whisper…"

Luis opened the first door he came to. It appeared to be an office. He saw a laptop on a desk, next to another radio. What was it with the radios in this house? He had no idea what this radio did, but suspected it was valuable. He unhooked the radio and the laptop and set them in the hallway. He went back and opened the desk drawers, but saw nothing but files and loose papers. He looked in the closet. It was mostly full of empty luggage. He cursed and moved to the end of the hall. He opened the door and saw it was a kid's room. He scanned it quickly. There was nothing but kid toys and other junk in there. He checked the next room and found another kid's room — worthless. He didn't even bother looking around, and slammed the door in disgust.

He walked to the doorway to the master bedroom at the end of the hall. He tried the door. It was locked. Now he knew where the woman and girl had gone.

Without another thought, he gave the door a sharp kick with his right foot, to the right side of the door, directly below the handle. With almost no resistance, the doorframe gave way, splintering as the door flew open. His body kept moving forward, since he'd put his body weight behind the kick. His right foot landed hard on the floor in front of him. As the door bounced off the doorstop and as Luis' momentum carried him forward, the door flew back the way it had come and smashed into his nose.

"Aaaaah!" Luis bellowed in rage and pain, both hands pressed over his nose, now gushing blood. Tears started to stream out of both eyes as he fell to his knees, trying to manage the blinding pain, while breathing through his mouth and choking up some of the blood that had started to drain down the back of his throat.

Luis was angry. This house was cursed, and the loot he'd gathered up so far was not even close to being worth the pain he'd suffered. In his agitated and confused state, it never occurred to Luis that he had inflicted all of this pain on himself. It was obviously the fault of the house and its inhabitants, even if they were hiding behind a locked door.

Holding his nose with one hand, and wiping tears of pain away with the other, Luis scanned the room. He needed to clean up the mess that was his face. He saw what must be the bathroom door and tried to open it. Locked. This was stupid. Much more carefully this time, he kicked the door in, but without placing himself in the door's return path. The door flew open, hit the doorstop, and only swung back about a foot.

Expecting the woman and girl to be inside, Luis was ready for a fight, but the bathroom was empty. He grabbed the nearest towel and held it against his nose, wincing at the light contact. He turned the faucet on over the sink. Nothing happened. He cursed. All his life, whenever he had turned a faucet, water had come out. He never understood how, but now that it had stopped, it added to his growing anger.

He still had a job to do here, and he allowed the anger and pain to drive him forward. He needed to get out of this cursed house, cash in the stuff he'd found, and get to an ER so they could fix his nose. They'd have to take care of him, he thought, looking in the mirror. He looked pretty bad, blood all over the front of his shirt.

He crossed the room, opened the drawer in the nightstand, and saw an MP3 player with headphones, which he stuffed into his back pocket. He walked to the nightstand on the other side of the bed, and opened the drawer — bookmarks and a package of post-it notes, earplugs. More junk. He slammed the drawer shut in disgust. He looked at the bookshelf: more books, and an open metal box with a key in the lock. He looked in the box. It was empty. He looked under the bed and found shoes and more books. These people couldn't be poor, but where were the goods? He looked back at the empty metal box and realized where the real valuables were. The lady had obviously taken all the gold or jewelry or stacks of cash or whatever had been in the box when she fled... into the closet. It was the last room in the house that he hadn't inspected. They had to be in there, along with the stuff that should be his. After all the pain this house had caused him, he deserved a rich reward.

He walked over quietly and tried the handle, thinking that he would surprise them when he opened the door. It was locked. Like every other door in this house. It was time for another swift kick.

Luis encountered many locked doors in his past, both exterior and interior. Every one of them had flown open when he kicked hard, right under the doorknob. Once in a while an exterior door would take more than one kick, but they all eventually gave way. Interior doors were even easier, barely requiring any force to smash open, and they were almost never locked anyway.

He pulled his right foot back, lifted his knee up toward his belly, and then powered his foot forward to the familiar destination, just below the doorknob.

The door didn't move, and a jolt of pain shot up his leg and his lower back. This was the last straw. He couldn't take it anymore, and the anger washed over him like a red, hot wave.

"Open the door now, or I'm going to kick it down!" he shouted. First he cut himself on their window, and he couldn't even climb through it. Then he wasted time breaking through an unlocked door. Then he was attacked by the bedroom door, and now the closet door was sitting there, quietly taunting him. He was done with this. It was clear that all of the best stuff in the house was locked behind this door. There was no way he was going to let a stupid woman get the best of him. He was going to win this fight, at any cost.

He tried to clear his head and think. Maybe he could convince them to open the door. They had to be terrified. Maybe he could make a deal with them.

"If you think I'm mad now, it's only going to get worse if you don't open the door. Just open up now and we can make a deal. I won't hurt you." He couldn't think of anything more clever to say.

Marie sat on a pile of laundry, with Lisa in her lap, wrapped in her arms. Lisa looked up at her mother, a tear running down her cheek. She was obviously very scared. Marie motioned to keep quiet with a finger to her lips. She silently mouthed "It'll be OK. Don't worry. He can't get in."

Luis kicked the door again, this time with his other foot. The thump was loud, and both Marie and Lisa jumped. The door didn't budge. Now his left foot hurt too. He cursed loudly. It didn't make any sense! What kind of door was this?

He thought for a minute, as he stood outside the room with clenched fists. "I'm gonna go down to the garage and get an axe or a bat or a shovel. You know I'll find something. And I'm going to chop through this door, and I'm going to get what I came for. This is your last chance to open up. I won't hurt you or the girl. Do it now!"

Marie and Lisa didn't move. They sat in silence.

Luis walked out of the bedroom and stomped down the stairs.

33. Back in the Neighborhood

Robbie drove down the side road toward a wider, arterial road, which should lead them almost all the way home. In this direction, toward the city instead of toward the highway, traffic was very light. In the other direction, it was starting to back up farther and farther into the city. The highway was more or less at a standstill now.

"It won't be long before these people run out of gas and get stranded," Jeff said. I'm glad we live a few miles from the highway, because these people will be looking for a place to stay and food to eat, and I'm not sure how much room we have at the moment. It'll probably get ugly."

They passed a gas station on their left. It was packed with cars, and a long line of cars extended into the road. Most of the people waiting were standing out of their cars. Some people stood in small groups, talking. Nobody seemed to be pumping gas, although one person was kicking one of the pumps and shouting. The convenience store and cash register area was dark, and they didn't see anyone inside.

"The clerks either shut down and went home, or they're hiding in there. They know that they can't sell anything without power. If they're in there, they're probably afraid to leave," Jeff said. "If the power doesn't come on soon, I bet that someone will break in to get food or something to drink. And once someone breaks their way in, everyone else will come in too. But they still won't get any gas." Robbie and Jeff continued down the road, leaving the gas station behind, with no desire to see the spark of frustrated, waiting, fearful people turn into a flame of looters and chaos.

"Turn right up there, right Dad?" Robbie asked.

"Yes. Take the turn slowly. We may have to keep going straight if it's a mess in that direction. We don't want to drive into another traffic jam and get stuck."

Robbie slowly turned the corner, ready to step on the brakes at any moment. The road was clear and he accelerated. They only had a few blocks to go.

Now they were passing a small shopping center, with a QFC grocery store in the middle. A line of people extended out of the store into the parking lot, and a man with a uniform stood at the entrance. He looked like a security guard, not one of the local police officers.

Robbie and Jeff saw a large, handwritten sign taped to a window. It read "Cash only[47]. $50 limit per family." Below that, in even larger print, was written "No credit cards, debit cards, or checks allowed!" They kept driving.

34. Home at Last

Robbie turned onto their street, Southeast Seventeenth Court, heart racing as he anticipated seeing his mother and sister soon. Jeff looked from side to side, scanning for damage in the neighborhood. He was relieved to there was very little visible damage. Their neighbors were probably relatively safe, and things might be back to normal here in a matter of weeks, even days.

"We're almost home, Dad!" Robbie said, excitement clear in his voice. "And it doesn't look that bad around here. This could be way worse." He realized that he had been hoping for this all day long, and now it seemed like things were finally getting better, even in the midst of this disaster.

"Yeah. This is good news. It looks like our neighborhood is in pretty good shape."

"How long do you think it will be before things are back to normal?" Robbie asked.

"No idea. Might be a few days. This was a big quake."

Robbie was quiet, thinking about his friends from school, wondering how they were doing, whether they were OK or maybe even homeless, or worse. He kept driving.

Standing silently in the closet, thinking about what to do next, Marie leaned against a shelf and felt something jab her in the side. It was the radio antenna. That's right! She had a radio with her!

Cursing silently, she took the radio off her belt, turned it on, and turned the volume almost all the way down, so the intruder wouldn't be able to hear anything.

The radio was set to a local repeater frequency. She tried it. "This is an emergency — can anyone hear me? I repeat — this is a life-or-death emergency — is anyone there?" she whispered fiercely. She released the transmit button and listened for a reply. Nothing. The repeater should have beeped. Of course! It should also be busy with emergency traffic. There were a lot of people in the area who used that repeater, and at least some of them should be talking. But there was nothing. The repeater was obviously down. Maybe a lot of the repeaters were down.

Marie remembered what she was supposed to do in an emergency. She changed frequencies, to the "2M Primary" channel that Jeff had programmed in earlier[48]. It would allow them to talk directly, without a repeater in between. She pressed the transmit button and hissed into the microphone again. "This is an emergency! Can anyone hear me? Jeff, are you out there? I need help!"

"…need help!"

Jeff and Robbie opened their mouths in surprise. Robbie slowed down instinctively as his brain raced to process what he heard. Yes, that was his mother. Once his brain caught up, Robbie pushed down hard on the accelerator. It was time to get home. Now.

Jeff was already transmitting a reply. "Marie, it's Jeff[49]. Are you OK? We're on our way home now! We're on 148th by the park. Tell me what's wrong!"

Robbie made his first high-speed turn as he rounded the corner onto their street, tires squealing.

"There's a man in the house, and he's trying to break into the closet in our bedroom. Lisa and I are in here and we're OK, but I don't know how long we'll be safe. Please help us!"

Jeff and Robbie could tell she was whispering, and Jeff whispered back.

"We're pulling up now. Is the man armed?"

"He's trying to smash the door in," Marie whispered back, voice breaking. Jeff could tell she was starting to cry.

"I'll be there in a few seconds babe. Hold on."

Robbie stopped in front of the house, slammed the transmission into "park", jumped out of the truck, and started running to the front door. Jeff had to exit the truck more carefully, in order to keep from falling down.

"Robbie, wait. Don't go inside!" he called, still trying to be quiet. As Robbie reached the front door and waited, Jeff hopped toward him as fast as he could, not bothering to retrieve the makeshift crutch that lay on the back seat. He checked his waistband as he got closer. The handgun was still in its holster. As he Jeff reached the front door, Robbie had already tried the doorknob and found it locked. He fumbled with the keys.

"Hold on," Jeff whispered. "Let me go in first. And unlock the door quietly."

"I'm back!" Luis shouted. "And I have a sledgehammer, so you might as well open the door. I'm going to get in anyway."

He raised the sledgehammer over his head and slammed it forward with all his strength, into the center of the door. It left an ugly dent, and that's when he realized that the door wasn't wood. He should have known when he kicked it twice. The stupid door was made of metal!

Luis wasn't aware that this door, doorframe, and lock were different than the other interior doors in the house. When Jeff and Marie did some minor remodeling three years ago, they decided to install an exterior door in a reinforced door frame, and equip it with a high-quality, exterior door lock and deadbolt. This door could not be kicked down like most other doors could. In fact, a sledgehammer probably wouldn't get through it. Not quickly, anyway. They were safe for the moment.

As the door swung open silently on well-oiled hinges, Jeff and Robbie heard a crash upstairs. In a fluid motion that resulted from years of practice, Jeff drew his handgun and held it close to his body, angled downward safely, with his index finger extended along the side of the pistol, above and to the side of the trigger.

There was a lot of information to process now, and his biggest concern was getting to his wife and daughter. But he needed to keep Robbie safe too.

Realizing he should have done this before opening the door, he turned back to Robbie. "Stay close, but don't go up the stairs. I may need your help, but only come up if I call for you. If I don't call for you in five minutes, run out of here and find help. Tell someone that there is an armed, dangerous intruder in our house. Got it?"

"I'll wait here until you call me," Robbie said. "If you don't call for me soon, I'll go get help." His heart was pounding so loudly now, he was concerned that the man upstairs would hear it.

Jeff pressed the transmit button again. "Marie, wait fifteen seconds and then tell him that you're coming out. I want you to distract him. Try talking to him for a few seconds. I'm going to turn my radio all the way down in a second, so that it doesn't give my position away, OK?"

"OK, I understand," Marie said. "I'll start talking to him in fifteens seconds. Wait — he has a sledgehammer now. Be careful!"

"OK, I'll be there in a few seconds. I'm turning my radio down now, so that I don't give away my position."

He turned down the volume on his radio and clipped it to his belt. Then he dropped his left hand to the other side of his waistband and retrieved his flashlight.[50] He held it alongside the pistol, but didn't turn it on.

"Open the door now!" Luis shouted, as he hefted the sledgehammer again. He had never known anger like this before. He was so frustrated with these girls and this stupid deathtrap of a house. He was going to smash through and finish this. Maybe he would even punish the woman for not letting him in. He hadn't decided yet. He swung the sledgehammer at the door handle.

The sledgehammer smashed down on the door handle again, and Marie and Lisa jumped.

Marie gently pushed Lisa out of her lap and squatted in front of her. "Lisa," she whispered. "Cover your ears and stay there." Then she started counting quietly to herself. "One, two, three, four…"

With both hands shaking almost uncontrollably now, she retrieved the handgun from the upper shelf. If the man started to make it past the door, she was going to defend herself and Lisa. She turned off the dim light, so that the intruder wouldn't be able to see her in the darkness. She knew that if he somehow made it through the door, he would be silhouetted in the doorframe, and would be an easy target. She stood with both hands holding the pistol in front of her, arms straight, finger off the trigger until she saw what she was going to shoot, just like she'd trained in the class she took last year.

"Nine, ten, eleven…"

Jeff heard the last shout Luis made, and the smash of the sledgehammer on the door handle. He started quietly up the stairs. He winced on every other step as he briefly placed weight on his injured ankle, but the pain didn't stop him. There was a madman up there intent on harming his wife and daughter and if Jeff had to climb the stairs on two broken ankles, he would do it. He noticed the pain, but he didn't care. He would not be stopped.

Robbie felt very alone, and tried to think about what he could do to help. He couldn't just wait there. He took his own flashlight out of his jacket pocket. The sun had almost set by now, and he needed to see what was in the room. He turned the switch at the head of the light, which set it to the dimmest setting, clicked the light on, and looked around the room. Right away, his eyes fell on the fireplace tools in their stand on the far side of the room.

In the distant bedroom above, he heard a grunt, a smash, and the sound of clattering metal.

When Jeff reached the top of the stairwell, he scanned right and left and saw nothing. It was getting dark, but he could tell that nobody else was in the hallway. And he knew the sound had come from the master bedroom, so he crept down the hall in that direction. The bedroom door was wide open. He stepped forward a foot at a time, looking at a bigger piece of the room each time, "slicing the pie". The closer he got to the doorway, the more of the room he was able to see.

"Fifteen," Marie counted to herself. She called out loudly, "OK, we're coming out. I'll open the door. Please stop hitting it. I'll unlock it." She reached forward and rattled the doorknob for good measure.

Luis could hardly believe his good fortune. Finally, things were back on track. He could clean up here and move on. He smiled with satisfaction. He knew all along that he would win in the end.

He set down the sledgehammer and pulled the kitchen knife from his waistband, in case the woman was up to something. He was ready. He saw the doorknob moving and waited.

Jeff stepped forward a few inches and saw a foot. He moved farther and then saw the leg, then most of a man, holding a knife but not doing anything.

With no doubt in his mind that the man was armed with a deadly weapon and that he intended to harm his family, Jeff stepped the rest of the way into the bedroom, and aimed his flashlight at the man's face, put a small amount of pressure on the rear switch. He shouted with his best drill-sergeant voice, "Stop! Drop the knife now! Do it now or I will shoot you!"

As Jeff shouted, Luis reacted instinctively, his surprise causing him to turn toward the sound. As his eyes locked on Jeff's dark silhouette, Jeff pressed the switch the rest of the way.

The flashlight worked like a strobe-light, throwing 400 lumens at about 10 times per second, a rate designed to disrupt a person's thought processes, especially when their eyes were already adjusted to the darkness. The tight beam caught Luis full in the face. He had been so intent on smashing through the door that he hadn't noticed Jeff approaching through the doorway.

"Drop the knife now!" Jeff shouted again, using the same tone of voice he'd heard his drill sergeant use in basic training. "Marie and Lisa, stay down!"

Luis was instantly blinded by the flashing light. He threw his left hand up to cover his eyes, but didn't drop the knife. In his surprise, he reacted with a natural stress response and gripped it even harder.

"I have a gun, and it's aimed right at you," Jeff boomed. "This is your last warning — drop the knife now!" His gun was aimed directly at the upper center of the man's torso, and the small, tritium-filled[51] vials that filled his night sights gave him a clear sight picture, even in the dim light.

Luis dropped the knife. For a millisecond, he wondered whether this man was a typical, pudgy yuppie, pretending to sound like a cop, but he immediately dismissed the thought. He could tell. In his core, he knew that this man wasn't pretending. Luis was done. He wanted out. It was time to quit. His anger dissolved and his meager reserves of remaining energy were now dedicated to getting the heck out of this house. It just wasn't worth it. This house was cursed.

Jeff kept shouting. "Marie - stay in there until I give you the all clear. There may be others. I'll let you know when it's safe." Then he asked, "Are you OK in there?"

"We're both OK," Marie replied loudly.

Jeff exhaled deeply. He hadn't realized that he was holding his breath, waiting for Marie to answer. Thank God. He could feel the relief flood through his body.

"I'll be back in a few. Stay there. You're safe."

"OK."

"You," Jeff said loudly to the man who stood by the door, who was now holding both hands straight up, doing his best to not get shot. "Put your hands on the back of your head. Slowly walk this way, and then slowly walk down the stairs. If you make any sudden movement, I will shoot you."

Luis slowly walked down the hall, and Jeff kept his sights on the man's torso, backing up slowly to keep at least a couple yards distance between them. He didn't want the man getting any crazy ideas about trying to grab the gun from him. Jeff took a step backward, then another. And then his ankle gave out.

35. Escape

With the unexpected collapse of one leg, Jeff fell backwards, landing hard on his backside. He wasn't used to falling this way, and the impact with the floor knocked the wind out of him.

Luis was accustomed to looking for weakness in people, and he noticed both the limp and the wince of pain on the man's face as he stepped backwards to keep his distance. Then the unthinkable happened. Out of the blue, the man fell down.

In the quarter of a second that Luis stood and watched, deciding what to do, he realized that the man hadn't dropped his gun. It was still aimed in his general direction. Even though the man was definitely surprised, distracted and in pain, running forward and snatching the gun from him was clearly out of the question. The man's finger was on the trigger and Luis knew that he would still probably be able to shoot him.

Luis thought quickly, probably more clearly and quickly than he ever had before. The gun pointing at him had cleared his mind, and he knew he was in serious trouble. He didn't want to get shot, and he didn't want to get handed over to the police. He knew he'd get a much stiffer prison sentence this time. He'd used a weapon, and it probably looked like he was trying to murder the lady and her girl, even if he was just angry and trying to get to the good stuff in the closet. Being on parole as he was would only make things worse. He was going to preserve his freedom.

Before the man realized what was happening, Luis leaped down the stairs. He took them three at a time and slammed into the wall halfway down as the stairs changed direction, going back down the other way. Luis turned and jumped down the next three stairs, close to the bottom now.

Robbie had been listening and watching intently, and he was shocked to see a man with a crazed look in his eyes bounding down the stairs toward him. He did the only thing he could think of. He raised his flashlight.

Out of nowhere, for the second time today, a blinding, flashing light seared Luis' brain. Not able to stop his forward momentum, and confused by the bright light, Luis misjudged where the next step was, tripped and crashed down the last several steps, sprawling onto the floor at the bottom of the stairs.

Luis felt a stabbing pain below his right knee and hoped it wouldn't slow him down. Fueled by his desire to escape, and his need to make that incredibly annoying light stop shining in his eyes, he stood up with most of his weight on his left leg. He could still walk. Still dazed by the flashing light and his recent tumble, he staggered toward it, both hands out, eyes closed to slits, trying to get closer. The light didn't move as he closed in.

Keeping the flashlight aimed at Luis' face, Robbie took a short step forward, squatted slightly and swung the fireplace poker in a wide, low arc, aiming at the leg that appeared to be injured. With a sharp "crack", the poker impacted right below the knee. Luis cried out and fell in a crumpled heap. He lay on the floor, writhing in pain, moaning and clutching his leg. This time he didn't attempt to get up.

Seconds later, Jeff finished hobbling down the stairs and leaned against the banister to steady himself, with his gun aimed at Luis.

"If you try to get up, I will shoot you!" he bellowed.

"I can't move. I can't walk," Luis cried.

"Good," Jeff said. "Be quiet and stay right there and you won't get hurt worse."

He looked at Robbie. "Are you OK?"

"Yeah."

"I'm sorry Robbie. I shouldn't have let him get away from me, and I put you in danger."

"It's all right, Dad. We got him, and I could run faster than him anyway."

They both stared at the man lying on the floor, clutching his leg and moaning.

"Go get a roll of duct tape from the garage. Be quick," Jeff said.

In less than a minute, Robbie returned with a gray roll. Jeff quickly applied several wraps of tape to the man's wrists, after pulling them behind his back.

Then he wrapped the tape around the man's ankles, trying not to move the injured leg more than necessary as Luis moaned in pain.

"Shut up. I'm helping you," Jeff said. He thought that securing the legs this way would actually reduce any more injury to the leg, since the healthy leg would act as a splint.

Now sure that the man was no longer a danger to anyone, Jeff searched his pockets and found his ID, some loose change, a small pocketknife, and his own MP3 player with headphones from his nightstand upstairs. "These look familiar." He set everything aside, and with Robbie's help dragged the man by his shoulders out onto the porch.

"It's OK" Jeff shouted up the stairs. "Marie and Lisa, you can come down now."

They heard the door unlock, heard pattering feet, and moments later, they were all together at the base of the stairs, hugging and crying.

"We're all safe now," said Jeff. "But we have a lot of work to do, including getting the police here as soon as possible, to take this sack of garbage off our porch. I'll radio someone on my ARES team — they'll be in contact with police. This guy can relax out there for a couple minutes in the meantime. You wouldn't believe the day we've had, even though nobody was actually trying to hurt us."

Wiping a tear from her eye, Marie said "There was no way he was going to hurt us. If he would have made it through the door or wall, I would have emptied the magazine into him."

"Glad to hear that. I'm married to a true warrior woman," Jeff said with a smile.

"You're married to a mom, that's all," Marie said, looking up at him with a smile. "Any mom would do what it takes to protect her child."

They hugged each other again, and stood embracing quietly for several seconds.

"Guess what Robbie did today?" Jeff said, changing the subject.

"What?" Lisa asked, clearly intrigued.

"He drove us home, sometimes going the wrong way on the highway. And sometimes backwards. Oh yeah, he also rescued me from the ledge I was stuck on, after I fell off of a cliff."

Marie and Lisa looked at him dumbfounded. They could tell he was serious. Marie actually had her mouth open. After their sixteen years of marriage, she didn't get surprised by his antics much anymore, but this time she was flabbergasted. She quickly regained her composure and closed her mouth.

"It sounds like you have some stories to tell," Marie said, beaming at Robbie.

"We do," Jeff replied, looking at Robbie, who was blushing now. "Today was a big day for a lot of reasons. But one of those reasons is that Robbie showed that he was a real man."

"Yay, Robbie's all growed up!" cried Lisa.

Robbie smiled and looked at his family, relieved and happy that they were all safe and together. In the back of his mind, he wondered what would happen next.

END

Bonus Content

Welcome to the bonus content section. You may have questions about ham radio, emergency preparedness, wilderness survival, and more. Get some answers here!

Also, go to **www.PreparedBlog.com** for more free, cool tips! You'll also be able to see any updates to this material, changes in Internet links, and other interesting content.

All items in this section are listed in the order they appear in the story, and you can also refer to the special table of contents to refresh your memory later.

Enjoy!

Table of Contents – Bonus Material

[1] **What should be in your backpack when you go on a hike?** The "Top Ten List" contains all of the essentials for wilderness survival. Everyone should always have these when going hiking in the wilderness, even just for a day trip. For overnight trips, a variety of additional supplies should be taken (for example, a sleeping bag), but this is a list of the minimum supplies needed.

Here is the list, with some examples you can research further. Of course, when you're hiking in the desert or the rain forest, there will be different needs, but this is a good starting point for most hikers:

- **Emergency Shelter**: A "bivvy-bag" (bivouac sack), plastic tube tent, lightweight tarp, poncho, large garbage bag, or Mylar blanket (space blanket).
- **Jacket**: It should have a hood, and be warm and waterproof (consider Gore-tex).
- **Fire starter**: Waterproof matches, stormproof lighter, ferrocerium rod, or magnesium block, and a backup.
- **Water**: At least one liter per person, with a way to filter and/or purify more. Depending on your location, you may need to carry two liters or more, even for a day trip.
- **Food**: Snacks, Clif Bars, MRE snacks, in addition to planned meals.
- **Map and compass**: A high-quality compass and topographical map.

- **Knife**: A sturdy, fixed-blade knife, if that's legal where you live. Otherwise, a lock-blade, folding knife will work.
- **Multi-tool**: An all-in-one tool (usually has pliers, a screwdriver, bottle opener, and more) made by a reputable manufacturer, like Leatherman, Gerber or SOG.
- **Whistle**: Many survival whistles can be heard from a great distance, and they weigh as little as a fraction of an ounce — there is no reason to not have one of these handy.
- **Flashlight**: Use an LED flashlight. Modern ones are very bright and the "bulbs" never burn out. Don't forget spare batteries.

What should you do with these items? Obviously, you will need to know how to use them. Make sure you do your research. But wait! There's more! One last thing — the most important thing you must have with you (and thank goodness you already have it screwed onto your shoulders): your head! If you don't know what to do with any of the items listed above, you need to learn. Your brain is the most important tool you have, and if you have the ability to think clearly and apply your knowledge to a dangerous and even life-threatening survival situation, you will be much better off.

[2] **What is ferrocerium?** Ferrocerium is a manmade, metallic substance that gives off sparks when scraped by a piece of steel. It is a great back-up fire-starter because it will work at high altitudes (where a lighter may not), and it won't run out of fuel. It'll eventually wear out, but you will be able to tell it's "running low" long before you scrape away all of the material. Also, you can get it wet, dry it off, and use it right away. The downside to using ferrocerium and similar fire-

starters is that you need to prepare the tinder carefully, to catch the sparks as they fall. With a lighter or matches, you can just hold the flame up to something flammable until it starts to burn.

As with anything dangerous, if you want to practice, make sure you have adult supervision!

[3] **What is ham radio?** It's the term used to refer to amateur radio, a fun hobby for many. But why "ham"? Some people speculate that it's because certain people involved in amateur radio back in the old days really loved to talk, and would "ham it up", telling long stories to their buddies when they'd get together on the airwaves to chat.

How does ham radio work? The Federal Communications Commission (FCC) has set aside certain frequencies for people to use for non-business-related communication. People use these frequencies to talk to each other using different kinds of radio equipment. Not only can you talk back and forth on these radios, you can also send text messages, transmit GPS coordinates, talk to repeaters, send and receive TV signals, bounce signals off of satellites or even the moon. Some people have even used hand-held radios to talk with the International Space Station! That's right — a person on the ground aims an antenna upward, tunes a radio to the right frequency, and has a conversation with an astronaut who is also a ham radio operator. Pretty crazy, right?

To use a radio that works on amateur radio frequencies, you need to take a simple test and get a license. The first license, called "Technician", is not difficult to get, and there are a many books, CDs, and websites available to walk you through the questions and answers. Once you've reviewed the material and feel comfortable, you can take a test and get your own license! Many ham radio clubs administer the tests, and will be happy to help you with the simple paperwork at the same time. Soon after, you'll get your call sign from the FCC, and you can get on the air!

These links will provide some additional, general information about ham radio: http://www.arrl.org/what-is-ham-radio-1, http://en.wikipedia.org/wiki/Amateur_radio.

[4] **How do call signs work?** After passing a licensing exam, a ham radio operator is issued a call sign by the FCC. The call sign is used to identify the person operating the radio whenever he is transmitting on ham frequencies. Since 1934, west of the Mississippi, call signs that start with "K" are issued, and east of the Mississippi, call signs that start with "W" are issued. If you listen to music on the radio in the car or at home, you will occasionally hear the station announce "This is KMPS" or "You're listening to WKRP" (or some other combination of letters) — this is their call sign, also issued by the FCC. Since the station is a business, their call sign is a slightly different format, but the idea is the same. When people talk on certain frequencies, they have to identify themselves with a call sign. When you get your license, you'll get your own call sign!

Do you want to look up a call sign? You can do that here: http://www.qrz.com/. If you're looking for more details, you could also try the FCC database directly. One easy way to do that is to go to http://wireless2.fcc.gov/UlsApp/UlsSearch/searchLicense.jsp. (And if that link changes, just go to www.fcc.gov, and search for the term "call sign search".)

[5] **Can you get your own call sign?** If you're willing to pay a few dollars extra, you can get a call sign with letters and numbers that you choose, called a "vanity call sign." And depending on the level of license that you choose to get, they

will be anywhere from four to six characters long. If you are able to get the "Extra" license, you can get a call sign with four, five, or six characters. Having a "General" license will allow you to use five or six characters. The "Technician" license will allow you to use six. If you prefer, you can keep the original six-character call sign issued by the FCC, regardless of what additional licenses you may get later. Here are some fun possibilities, combining different characters: N0HOW, K1SS, K0RN, W0MAN, WA5HME, and KN1TTR. When it's your turn, you choose!

[6] **What is GPS?** The Global Positioning System is a satellite-based navigation system. It allows a device to receive satellite signals and use them to determine its position. In the past, the receivers were expensive, slow to find a location, and less accurate. Nowadays they are fast and you can find them in cars, cell phones, and ham radios. The GPS system used to be accurate within 100 meters (300 feet), but in the year 2000 the U.S. Government turned on a feature that allowed everyone to get data that is accurate within 20 meters (65 feet).

[7] **What is "APRS"?** The letters APRS stands for Automatic Packet Reporting System, a system developed by Bob Bruniga, whose call sign is WB4APR. (In case you're wondering why the call sign matters, ham guys like you to know what their call sign is in case you come across it on the airwaves sometime.) It's an interesting, flexible, and useful system that allows users to transmit text messages, alerts, bulletins, etc., in addition to their GPS coordinates.

You might be able to imagine how handy this system would be for people on search and rescue missions or during other emergencies, aside from during everyday communications. Here are two places to learn more about APRS:

---

http://en.wikipedia.org/wiki/Automatic_Packet_Reporting_Syst
em and http://www.aprs.org.

[8] **What is the "Half-tank rule?"** It's very simple: Never let
your gas tank get less than half-empty. When your gas gauge
shows half-empty, fill it up again. Why do this? You'll never
run out of gas. And in the event that you aren't able to go to a
gas station and fill up due to some unexpected circumstances,
you'll still have plenty of gas to get where you're going. Time
after time, people are caught off guard in snowstorms, get lost
in a new place, or even drive down the highway somewhere
close to home and run out of gas, which puts them in a
dangerous situation. It's very easy to prevent that with the
"Half-tank rule."

[9] **Topographic maps** are very useful when travelling in the
wilderness. Why? Because they show important features that
roadmaps don't. Topographic maps show roads, but also show
trails, even old, unmaintained trails, as well as changes in
elevation. If you know how to read a topographic map, you can
look at the lines and determine whether the trail goes uphill or
downhill. You'll be able to see if there is a cliff or a mountain
next to you. And in the wilderness, this is very important,
because there are very few road signs! You can use the
topography to help pinpoint your location, and determine how
much work you still have left to do before you reach your
destination. If you are going hiking or camping in the
wilderness, you should purchase (or download and print) and
learn how to read a topographic map.

[10] The acronym **MRE** stands for "**M**eal, **R**eady to **E**at."
They are quick and simple. An MRE is usually packaged as a
full meal, including a main dish, crackers or bread, and some
kind of spread like peanut butter, cheese or jam. They usually
contain a snack, dessert, spoon, gum, salt, pepper, instant

coffee, cream, sugar, and even toilet paper. Newer MRE's have a special heater (if they are the military style) which is activated by pouring a small amount of water into a plastic bag, which can be used to heat the food when the weather is cold. (Some MRE main dishes taste much better warm than cold!) MRE's can be stored for up to three years at 80 degrees Fahrenheit, although they can last for years longer than that, if they are stored at lower temperatures. Although they are heavier than freeze-dried backpacking meals, they are quite handy because they don't require any cooking or boiling water.

In recent years, it has become very difficult, if not impossible, to obtain surplus military MRE's, although they are available legally from various distributors. For short-term, easy-to-prepare, high-calorie meals that require no additional water or preparation, MRE's are hard to beat!

[11] **How does a repeater work?** The quick version:

1. You transmit a message with your radio.
2. The repeater receives the message.
3. The repeater simultaneously (only a tiny fraction of a second later) re-broadcasts that message, usually with much more power and range.

This is especially useful when using a low-power, handheld radio. Through a repeater, a little radio can transmit and receive across a huge territory. Cool!

[12] **What are tone and offset and how do they matter?**
Many repeaters listen for a special **tone**, which is included in the signal that carries your voice when you transmit your spoken words. Usually this is programmed into your radio when you set up the frequency to use with the repeater. Without that special tone, the repeater won't repeat what you transmitted.

The **offset** tells your radio what distance to move up or down the frequency spectrum, in order to order to match what the repeater will receive and transmit. For example, a repeater will receive a signal on 146.**050** megahertz (MHz), and then re-transmit that same signal on 146.**650** MHz. This means that when you use your radio, you will press the transmit button, your radio will transmit your voice on 146.050 MHz, the repeater will receive your transmission, and then it will re-transmit it on 146.650 MHz.

[13] **How can you see a radio on a computer map?** Many people and vehicles use APRS to broadcast their location. Their radios act as beacons, and they can be seen online here: http://aprs.fi. (Give it a minute to load – you may have a lot of data to show in your area.) This map provides up-to-date, accurate location information showing people, vehicles, boats, etc., as they continuously transmit packets of GPS data to other APRS-compatible radios. Take a look and see for yourself.

You can see a recent snapshot of APRS activity across the U.S. here, from late 2010: http://www.aprs.org/maps/USA-Turkey-10.png. As you can see, most of the APRS traffic takes place in urban areas or near highways, but plenty of people in rural areas use APRS too.

[14] **Are amateur radio conversations private?** No. Ham radios operate on frequencies that are public, so anyone can listen. If you don't want anyone to hear what you're talking about, you should use a phone or email instead. Also, if you're thinking about using a secret code when you talk on the radio, don't. It's against the FCC rules to disguise or "obfuscate" (a fancy word for encoding or hiding) your conversation.

[15] **Are you aware of what natural disasters may occur in your area?** You'll need to have this information if you're

going to be able to prepare effectively. For example, depending on where someone in Washington State lives, he may be concerned about a dam breaking, an earthquake, a volcano erupting, a tsunami, flooding rivers, wildfire, avalanche or mudslide. Do you live in "Tornado Alley"? Is your city built on a geological fault line? You can find more information from your local Red Cross office as well as your local government emergency management office.

[16] **What is 550 cord?** It's lightweight nylon rope made up of a nylon sheath and seven internal nylon cords. The "550" is a reference to its breaking strength of 550 pounds. 550 cord is so handy that some people even wear bracelets made out of it so that they'll always have some available just in case!

[17] **Everyone should know basic first aid and CPR.** However, you probably shouldn't attempt first aid techniques if you've never actually been trained on how to do them properly. If you make a mistake, you could accidentally make a person's injuries even worse! There are many options available for taking a certified, safe first aid course.

The Red Cross commonly offers several different courses, and there are probably at least first aid and CPR courses available in your area. You could also check with your local hospital or fire department.

Why take first aid and CPR? Because people you know could hurt themselves, maybe even seriously, and you should be able to help! You may even save someone's life.

Neat Trick: one "tool of the trade" you may learn about in a basic first aid course is a technique to determine whether a splint is too tight: you give a toenail or fingernail of the splinted limb a little squeeze. If the pink/red color (which is blood flowing back to the area) of the nail comes back quickly, that means you are probably getting enough blood flow in that area. If the color stays white or light pink and doesn't darken again, then blood isn't flowing as quickly as it should, and you may need to loosen the ties on the splint in order to prevent even more damage to the wounded area. But remember, this book is not a first aid course – go take a real course with your local Red Cross! Here is where you can find American Red Cross class information: http://www.redcross.org/en/takeaclass.

[18] **What's in your first aid kit?** Here are some interesting options you may not be aware of:

- **Celox® and QuickClot®** are two different brands of "hemostatic granules" and a variety of bandages, sponges, etc., which are used to cause very quick and reliable clotting in a bleeding wound. These granules are commonly poured directly into a bleeding wound to cause a clot, in order to stop life-threatening bleeding.
- An Israeli medic named Bernard Bar-Natan invented a trauma bandage, often simply referred to as an **"Israeli Trauma Bandage,"** which can be relatively easily put on with one hand and will apply enough pressure to stop many kinds of bleeding.
- SAM Medical® sells a popular splint known as a **"SAM splint,"** made of a foldable sheet of aluminum encased by thin foam. The splint can be easily molded to fit any angle of the body, and can be tied down to help immobilize an injury.

[19] **Consider an advanced first aid course.** Have you taken a first aid course, but are looking for more training? You have more options. You may find a "Wilderness First Aid" course in your area, which will provide some additional, different techniques than what you might get from a regular first aid course. These techniques will be especially helpful if an injury

occurs out in the wilderness, like when you are hiking or camping, not near any roadway where you could be quickly transported to a clinic or hospital.

If you want to get even more advanced training, you could take a course like the Red Cross "First Responder" course. In this course, not only do you learn some advanced techniques for CPR and rescue breathing, but even more advanced first aid techniques, and even how to help get someone safely out of a vehicle after a crash.

For adults, there are also opportunities to get Emergency Medical Technician (EMT) training. You may be able to volunteer with a local fire department or other public service group to keep your skills up-to-date. Opportunities vary depending on your location. If you're interested in becoming an EMT, you can start by asking at your local fire department, or possibly a school in the area that teaches an EMT course.

[20] **What is NOAA? NOAA** stands for the **N**ational **O**ceanic and **A**tmospheric **A**dministration, and is part of the U.S. Department of Commerce. That may sound pretty boring, but there are many times when their messages are very interesting! When bad weather, natural disasters, and other life-threatening hazards happen, NOAA's National Weather Service makes special announcements on certain radio frequencies, using one or more of their 1000+ radio stations across the country. Each station covers a small area by design, because announcements only matter for specific area.

NOAA also regularly broadcasts weather forecasts on these frequencies. Certain radios receive only these frequencies, and are often called "weather radios". Many ham radios, and some FRS/GMRS radios (the kind of handheld radios you can get at the sporting goods store) will also receive these frequencies.

Some of these radios listen for emergency announcements, and will alert the user when it hears them. You can find more information on www.weather.gov/nwr.

[21] **What is CERT?** The Community Emergency Response Team (CERT) Program educates people about disaster preparedness for hazards that may take place in their area and teaches basic disaster response skills, such as fire safety, basic search and rescue, team organization, and disaster medical operations. The training includes time in the classroom and some exercises, such as putting out real fires (controlled, of course) with a fire extinguisher! After completing the training, CERT members are better prepared to assist people in their neighborhood or workplace if a disaster happens, especially if there are no police officers or firefighters available to help. You can find more information at http://www.citizencorps.gov/cert/.

[22] **Do you know how to shut off your water, natural gas, and electricity?** If you hear the hissing of natural gas or see water gushing from a broken pipe in your house, that's the wrong time to start wondering where your shutoff valve is. If you know that electrical wires are arcing or sparking, you will need to shut off the power switch at your breaker box. Do you know where it is? Do you know how to shut off your main breaker?

If you haven't already, you should locate your breaker box, gas and water shutoff valves. In addition, you will need to make sure you have the right tools to turn those valves.

[23] **Don't turn your gas back on!** If you ever need to turn off your natural gas (by turning the valve off at the meter) because you suspect a leak, don't turn it back on. Let someone from the gas company come by and inspect your line and turn the gas back on. Even a small gas leak could result in an

explosion, and it only takes a small spark (for example, using a cell phone or an electrical switch) to set it off. Let an expert inspect your system.

[24] **How can you run your handheld radio using regular AA batteries?** If you don't have a special adapter, you won't be able to! But you should have one of these adapters for any handheld radio. AA batteries (alkaline, lithium, and rechargeable) are widely available, and you may have them handy in an emergency situation when you may not have power available to recharge your regular battery.

AA battery adapters for handheld radios take the place of the regular rechargeable battery. The disadvantage with these adapters in some cases is that you may not be able to transmit with the same maximum power as you could with your regular battery. For example, with the Yaesu VX-8R, the rechargeable lithium ion battery will allow a maximum five Watts of transmission power, while the AA battery pack (part# FBA-39), which holds three AA batteries, will allow a maximum of only one Watt.

[25] **What's the deal with the special words?** Do you have to say "monitoring" or "clear" when using a ham radio? There are words that hams commonly use to indicate what they're doing. If they sign off, they often say "clear." When they say "clear and monitoring", this usually means that someone wants to be done with the conversation, but he will still keep his radio on and listen to it. Amateur radio has plenty of special terms, like in any hobby.

If you want to get an old ham all riled up, get on the radio and say "10-4 good buddy," like people used to say on their CB radios in 70's movies. Any words that sound like CB talk will make most ham radio operators squirm.

Another thing you may notice if you listen to the radio for a while is that many ham operators like to us "Q-codes." These are special "brevity" codes that all start with the letter "Q". These codes come in handy when transmitting in Morse code, because the operator can condense several words into just a few letters. However, some of these hams like to use their Q-codes when speaking also. For example, they'll say "What's your QTH" instead of "What's your location?" As you can see, each term has three syllables, so nobody is saving much time with that one. If you don't know any of these codes, that's no problem — just talk normally and everyone will understand what you mean!

[26] **Are you ready for an emergency?** One measure you can use is the Red Cross checklist — a set of topics that will help you determine whether you meet their readiness criteria. The list covers these main topics: know what emergencies or disasters are most likely to occur in your area, have a family disaster plan (and practice it), have an emergency preparedness kit, get trained in first aid and CPR, take action to help your community prepare. You can get more information at www.redcross.org.

[27] **What happens to tap water after an earthquake?** You should be prepared for a variety of scenarios that result in your fresh tap water not being available, because of broken pipes, pumps that stop working, or contamination. In any of those cases, you should already be prepared with stored water. Five-gallon water cans are good for water storage, and are much more portable than barrels.

[28] **Will cell phone and landline phones work after an earthquake?** You shouldn't count on any phones working. Cell phone towers require power to operate. Even if they have backup power from batteries and generators, the batteries will

eventually drain and generators can 1) break down or 2) run out of fuel. If a cell tower is still working, you should still not expect that a call will get through, simply because so many people will be trying to use it at the same time. What's your best bet for using your cell phone? Send a text message! Text messages take up far fewer resources and are more likely to reach their destination when cell tower traffic is extremely heavy.

Landlines (the phone systems people have been using for the last century) could also fail. Switching equipment and other gear essential to operate the telephone system also depended on electrical power. Another potential issue that may exist after an earthquake, even when power is still connected to the phone system: too many phones will have fallen off their hooks. When that happens, the switching systems can be overloaded, and to prevent further damage, large sections will be automatically shut off. If you have a landline, make sure to put the phone back in the cradle after an earthquake.

[29] **Will your local fire department be able to help after an earthquake?** Maybe, but probably not right after a big quake. Many fire stations in large cities (including the Seattle area) are of older construction, and will not fare well in an earthquake. Another concern unique to fire stations is that their large doors may be jammed, trapping fire engines inside. Of course, many roads will be impassable, water resupply may be impossible, and other problems will arise. In any case, don't expect that a fire truck will be on its way soon to any particular burning building right after an earthquake.

[30] **What can you do with a scanner?** You can listen to some interesting conversations. Most police, fire departments, buses, and other public services use radios to communicate. Since radios are more reliable than cell phones in many cases,

and will work in some areas where cell phones won't, this allows these organizations to have a constant, reliable way to communicate.

Most of these radios (with very few exceptions) operate on frequencies that you can listen to. That means you can listen to a police officer calling back to the dispatch center on his radio, asking for more information on someone he has pulled over. You can listen to a bus driver in a snowstorm, describing how certain roads aren't safe anymore. You can listen to a fire truck being called out, maybe even to an address in your neighborhood.

Scanners are designed to very quickly scan hundreds or thousands of frequencies, and will stop on one when there is a transmission in progress. Since police, firefighters, etc. aren't constantly talking on the radio, this will allow you to go where the action is. Of course, you can stay on a certain frequency if you like, in order to hear the rest of the conversation.

In amateur radio, most radios can very quickly scan lists of frequencies, or entire ranges of frequencies, between upper and lower limits that the radio can receive. They usually aren't as well-suited for scanning public-service transmissions, though.

One of the best and easiest to use is the Uniden Homepatrol, which was released in 2010. If you're interested in scanning, this is one of the easier ways to get started.

[31] **What are the three things you need to do to prepare for a disaster?** There are a few variations of this list, but they are essentially the same:

> 1. **Have a plan**: know what disasters you may face, and discuss your plans with your family.

    2.   **Have a kit** (or a variety of kits): Have at least three days of food and water stored, along with other emergency supplies you might need.

    3.   **Stay informed**: Know where to listen for additional information, e.g., a NOAA radio.

The Red Cross and Ready.gov versions look like this: "Get a kit, make a plan, and be informed." The "3 Days 3 Ways" version: "Make a plan, build a kit, and get involved." FEMA (Federal Emergency Management Agency) shows a similar list. You get the picture.

Additional resources: www.PreparedBlog.com, www.Ready.gov, www.RedCross.org, www.3days3ways.org.

[32] **Get involved with your community!** Whether you plan for it or not, your neighbors will affect your situation. If they aren't prepared, are you prepared to help them? Do you have extra food stored for your neighbors? If a neighbor comes over and asks "Can you spare a gallon of water? My kids are thirsty and my little boy is sick," what will you say?

Have you met your neighbors? Do you know whether you have a doctor, a police officer, or a mechanic living nearby? Could a neighbor take care of your pets if you need to leave? Could you take care of their pets? Could you relay any emergency messages for them, for example, if someone needs a special medication but can't leave the house?

Knowing your neighbors is a good thing. Aside from being able to keep any eye on your home if you're on vacation, there will be other opportunities to help each other, and you will be able to accomplish much more together than you will alone.

[33] **Learn some basic knots!** Knot-tying is a valuable skill, in the woods, at home, just about anywhere you might have a

piece of rope, cord, or string handy. Most knots are very easy to tie, if you practice. Nowadays you can find many websites that will show you how to tie them, and you can always get a book with illustrations. Here are the names of some of the most common, useful knots: overhand, figure-eight, square (reef), sheet bend, bowline, and clove hitch. There are many more. Go get a piece of rope and try some!

[34] **How can a Leatherman tool be useful?** There are many uses! Let's take the Leatherman Charge as an example. It has these features: knife blade, saw, file, serrated blade with hook, needle-nosed pliers, regular pliers, wire-cutters, a variety of small and large slotted and Philips-head screwdrivers, a bottle/can opener, and a ruler printed on the outside. Wow! You can do a lot of things with a tool like this. Your imagination is the only limit. Have you ever seen the *Survivorman* TV show? Survival guru Les Stroud has said more than once that if you can only have one thing with you in a survival situation, it should be a multi-tool.

[35] **Where will you go in an emergency?** In this case, it's easy for Jeff to determine that they need to go home. But what if they got home and his wife and daughter were not home because it was destroyed? Where would they be? In your family, do you have an agreed-on meeting location where you can go if you aren't able to communicate? If going home isn't an option, what is "Plan B"? Having a main and backup meeting location is an important part of any emergency plan.

[36] **Do you want to be a lumberjack?** If you ever have the occasion to cut down a tree with a chainsaw or axe, you must 1) learn how to use the tool from someone who knows what they're doing (*especially* with the chainsaw) and 2) always keep safety in mind! Many trees weigh thousands of pounds, and if a tree needs to move, no matter how strong you are, you

won't be able to stop it. Even if a tree is lying on the ground, it still may be dangerous. Bent branches bent holding up the thousands of pounds of tree trunk could snap, and if you're nearby, you could be seriously injured or killed. So of course, don't cut down a tree for no good reason, and if you need to actually chop one down or cut one into pieces, pay close attention and do it under the supervision of an expert. Learn how to do it safely; don't risk your life!

[37] **Do you have a plan for "getting out"?** "Get out of where?" you may ask. Good question. That depends on where you are, of course.

Are you at home? If you need to evacuate in an emergency, where will you go and how will you get there? Do you have a 3-day bag that will allow you to survive on the road (or sidewalk, or path) while you make you way somewhere else?

Are you at school or work? How will you get home? Are you on a road trip? How will you get home? Do you have three days of food, water, protection from the weather/environment, etc.? Do you have to travel on the road in an area that sometimes has blizzards? Could you survive on the side of the road for a day or two if you got stuck?

What should be in your bag? There are many lists of supplies, and your list depends on where you live and what your goal is. If you work a half mile from home, your "Get home bag" may be small or even nonexistent. As long as you have a good pair of shoes, that may be all you need. Think about what you need to accomplish before you pack a huge back full of camping supplies.

For more ideas on how to prepare to get from point A to point B, go online and look up these terms: *Bug-out bag, get-home bag, GOOD (Get Out Of Dodge) bag, three-day bag.*

You will find a variety of lists, and probably some great ideas you haven't thought of.

[38] **Should you evacuate a disaster area?** Maybe not. You may have food and clean water, a way to heat your home if needed, batteries for flashlights, and a radio that allows you to communicate with family and friends. It may be too dangerous to try to leave. For example, if most roads are seriously damaged or blocked, trying to evacuate might only place you in more danger. Staying home may be your safest option.

You could hear an announcement requesting people to "shelter-in-place" instead of evacuating. In addition to preparing a plan for evacuating, you should plan for staying home. For more information on sheltering-in-place, visit www.Ready.gov and www.redcross.org/preparedness.

[39] **What is the ARRL?** The Amateur Radio Relay League is a national association for amateur radio in the USA. (Other countries have similar associations.) At the time of this writing, it has about 150,000 members, and it provides books, news, support, and all kinds of other information for individuals, clubs and other organizations, and special events.

One great benefit of being a member of the ARRL is their monthly magazine, called *QST*, which is a great way to see what's new, learn about new technology and equipment, contests, and more. (QST is a "Q-code" which stands for "Calling all stations").

If you are interested in amateur radio, join the ARRL! You can find more information at www.arrl.org.

[40] **How can people communicate in an emergency? What is "EMCOMM"?** In many disasters, our fragile communications systems (telephones, cell phones, the Internet)

may fail or get overloaded with calls for help. In these cases, amateur radio will still work. Amateur radio operators can talk back and forth with each other directly with no need for other communication infrastructure. In many disasters around the world, ham radio operators have risen to the occasion and used their skills and applied their Emergency Communications (EMCOMM) training to make sure critical messages were passed along between individuals, emergency services agencies, and governments when no other communications options were available.

[41] **What are ARES and RACES?** ARES is an amateur radio emergency communication program in the U.S. This program has groups of ham radio operators who volunteer to help local and federal agencies during times of crisis and natural disasters. If you're interested in learning about emergency communications, consider joining an ARES group in your area. The dedicated and helpful volunteers that make up these groups would be happy to tell you more about how to participate.

ARES stands for Amateur Radio Emergency Services, and its training is sponsored by the ARRL (Amateur Radio Relay League). For more information, see: http://www.arrl.org/ares

RACES is a more formal organization, chartered by the FCC (Federal Communications Commission). RACES stands for Radio Amateur Civil Emergency Service. For more information, see: http://www.usraces.org/

[42] **What's a radio net?** When a group of people communicate on the radio in an organized fashion, it's usually called a "net". Some nets are more organized than others (an organized net usually has a "net controller", a person who calls to each person, asking for them to check in, etc.) Some nets are

less organized and participants chat freely. As the size of the group increases, however, more organization is usually necessary to keep everyone from talking at the same time, talking over each other. If you have a scanner or an amateur radio, you can listen to these nets. Contact your local ham radio club to learn more about nets that take place in your area. If you use an HF radio, you may be able to hear nets that take place hundreds of miles away, or even farther.

[43] **What is "Mike and Key"?** The Mike and Key Amateur Radio Club is a ham radio club in Renton, WA, active for over 40 years. There are hundreds of amateur radio clubs across the U.S., and many more in countries around the world. These clubs are a fantastic resource for new and experienced amateur radio and emergency communication enthusiasts. If you are interested in ham radio or new to ham radio, join a club!

Why? You can learn a lot. These clubs are full of people who have many years of experience. You can often find people who have several decades of experience. These club members are involved in many other activities you may find interesting, from helping at public service events (e.g., passing on messages at a marathon) and owning and managing repeaters, to participating together on "Field Day" and other contests (when radio operators get on the air at the same time to log contacts with each other, often all around the world). Being part of an amateur radio club is a great way to learn and participate in a variety of amateur radio activities.

[44] **If you have a gun in your home, it needs to be secured!** This means nobody is able to access it unless you allow it. You may choose a trigger lock, a locked box, or a gun safe. Many people who keep a weapon in the home for self-defense want to be able to access it quickly in an emergency. In cases like these, many people keep a handgun in a locked box that can be

opened quickly, either with a key or a biometric device, usually a fingerprint reader.

[45] **What kind of behavior should you expect in a disaster or other emergency situation?** We'd all like to think that people will act civilly with each other, wait in line, share, and use their manners. But in many cases this may not happen, and you should be prepared for this possibility.

You may be able to imagine the attitude of a mother who is anxious to get home as soon as she can, to see if her children are safe. To take it a step further, imagine a mother who wants to get home because she already knows her children are in danger or even injured. In this case, traffic laws may seem far less important to her, and waiting in a long line of traffic to merge with other traffic in an orderly manner may become an incredibly frustrating experience.

Imagine a father whose family hasn't had a meal for an entire day. His neighbors are out of food, and his wife and children are asking "Can you find us some food?" This man will probably consider breaking some rules in order to find food for his family. He may even steal or loot.

A British farmer came up with the expression "9 meals from anarchy" to describe a situation where supply chains were broken and supermarket shelves were bare for three days. In this situation, he and others predicted that law and order would start to break down and society would quickly descend into chaos. (It's hard to imagine a disaster in the USA where we don't have the support of local, state, and federal governments, which would result in convoys of clean water, food, medicine and other supplies being provided to the needy masses. Even so, having several days of your own supplies stored "just in case" is a good idea.)

In an emergency situation, turn up your level of awareness and be on the lookout for high-stress or irrational behavior. People will not act the way they normally do, especially if they are desperate for whatever reason.

[46] **Zip ties — what are they good for?** If you thought duct tape was the best all-around tool to have in every toolbox, you're still right. But zip-ties are also super-handy for many uses, from reattaching a license plate if the frame breaks to holding bunches of wires together neatly. Police even sometimes use special zip-ties as disposable handcuffs. Zip-ties don't take up much space, are easy to apply quickly, and are generally quite strong. As small and light as they are, you should definitely have some in all of your repair and tool kits.

[47] **Cash is king!** You should always have some cash handy. If the power goes out, you won't be able to use your credit or debit cards. You should also expect that many merchants will not accept a check as payment.

You don't need to have thousands of dollars in a coffee can in your kitchen cupboard, but at least a few ten- and twenty-dollar bills will come in handy if you need to buy something, even if it's from your neighbor.

[48] **Which channels do you have programmed in your radio?** If you have a ham radio, you might as well be prepared to use it in an emergency! One of the most important things you can do is have a plan for who you will talk to, when you will talk, and the frequency on which you will talk. (Of course, you can always communicate using digital modes over your computer, but we'll talk about that another time.)

Make sure you assign labels to certain frequencies as part of your emergency communication plan, before any emergency! For example "Main home" or "Backup home" (in case the first frequency you plan to talk on is very busy). In addition, make sure that the people you plan to talk with also have these frequencies and labels programmed in their radios.

[49] **What happened to the fancy radio-talk?** Why aren't they using their call signs? In this case, Jeff and Marie aren't worried about following amateur radio protocol. If you're in a life-or-death situation and need to use a ham radio, don't worry about the FCC. Just get on the radio and use it!

[50] **Do you need a flashlight?** A flashlight is a great tool for many reasons, even if you don't need to disorient a burglar (hopefully, you'll never need to do anything like that!). You can find a wide variety of small, pocket-sized flashlights that will allow you to see where you're going in an emergency at night, if the power goes out, if you're exploring a cave, or if you're looking around your attic or crawlspace. You might want a small light as part of your pocket carry kit. There are many options, from micro-lights that run on a single watch battery; to small, bright lights that run on a single AAA battery; to super-bright lights that run on two or more larger, lithium batteries. And LED's (Light-Emitting Diodes, the high-tech "light bulb" used in most modern flashlights) last so long, they almost never burn out. Some LED's are rated to produce light for 150,000 hours. That's 6,250 days — over 17 years. Yeah, that's a long, long time. But you'll need a *lot* of batteries to run it that long, so make sure you have spares!

[51] **What is tritium? Why is it so unusual?** Tritium is a radioactive isotope, and it is put into small vials that are inserted into "night sights", which are most often used in handguns. In low light or darkness, these small vials glow enough to see easily, which allows someone to accurately put their sights on a target when they might not be able to see them

clearly otherwise. This is very important because guns are frequently needed when the light is low or when it's dark.

You might wonder "Will this radioactive stuff kill me? What if I dig some out and play with it?" Tritium is completely safe. It's been tested and re-tested and it has been proven that the particles can't get past your outer layer of skin. Theoretically, you could possibly hurt yourself if you eat a lot of it, but you could also hurt yourself by eating many other things you shouldn't, so be smart and be careful, and don't eat tritium!

Tritium is also used on watch and compass faces, so that you'll be able to tell the time and navigate in low light or darkness.

Tritium has a half-life of 12.3 years, which means that in 12.3 years it will emit half as many particles as it does today — it will be half as bright. If you bought your watch or compass or night sights recently, you should be able to expect 10+ years of reliable glowing.

Made in the USA
Lexington, KY
19 May 2014